(TH)INGS
and
(TH)OUGHTS

Alla Gorbunova

TRANSLATED BY ELINA ALTER

DEEP VELLUM PUBLISHING

DALLAS, TEXAS

Deep Vellum Publishing
3000 Commerce Street, Dallas, Texas 75226
deepvellum.org · @deepvellum

Deep Vellum is a 501c3 nonprofit literary arts organization founded in 2013 with the mission to bring the world into conversation through literature.

Originally published in Russian as *Вещи и ущи* by Limbus Press, St. Petersburg, Russia, 2017

First English edition, 2025

The publication of the book was negotiated through Banke, Goumen & Smirnova Literary Agency (www.bgs-agency.com)

Support for this publication has been provided in part by grants from the Texas Commission on the Arts, the City of Dallas Office of Arts and Culture, the Communities Foundation of Texas, and the Addy Foundation.

ISBNs: 978-1-64605-403-9 (paperback) | 978-1-64605-404-6 (ebook)

LIBRARY OF CONGRESS CATALOGING-IN-PUBLICATION DATA
Names: Gorbunova, Alla, 1985- author | Alter, Elina translator
Title: (Th)ings and (th)oughts / Alla Gorbunova ; translated by Elina Alter.
Other titles: Veshchi i ushchi. English
Description: Dallas, Texas : Deep Vellum Publishing, 2025.
Identifiers: LCCN 2025021638 (print) | LCCN 2025021639 (ebook) | ISBN 9781646054039 trade paperback | ISBN 9781646054046 ebook
Subjects: LCGFT: Short stories
Classification: LCC PG3491.96.R3686 V4713 2025 (print) | LCC PG3491.96.R3686 (ebook) | DDC 891.73/5--dc23/eng/20250506
LC record available at https://lccn.loc.gov/2025021638
LC ebook record available at https://lccn.loc.gov/2025021639

Cover art and design by Sarah Schulte
Interior layout and typesetting by KGT

Praise for Alla Gorbunova

OTHER BOOKS BY ALLA GORBUNOVA AVAILABLE IN ENGLISH TRANSLATION

It's the End of the World, My Love

CONTENTS

II. THE WAY TO THE GALLOWS RUNS THROUGH MERRY MEADOWS

III. THE TRIALS OF IVAN PETROVICH   139

IV. ἐκπύρωσις (EKPYROSIS)

I

SONGS OF THE BLIND BEGGARS

PSYCHOANALYSIS IN HELL

Many people who, after death, find themselves in Hell, turn to psychologists, psychotherapists, and psychoanalysts, since being in Hell causes them to develop neuroses. I myself work in Hell as an analyst, and in my practice I often see patients who claim that they were decent people who never hurt anyone, and the very fact that they are now in Hell is, for them, a source of confusion and torment. It is specifically to this category of patient that I address my text. I've compiled a short memo outlining the best way to behave in these difficult circumstances.

I.   First, please don't assume that being in Hell is your fault, that it means you were a bad person, a sinner. Please don't assume that you deserve to be here, or that there's some unfathomable logic to all of this. No one can tell you why you wound up here. No one can tell you how to get out of here, either. The analysts are in Hell too, just like you are. Therefore, try to take a simple view of what's happening. You're in Hell. That's a fact.

This is a bad place. But there's no need for you to explain or interpret, trying out one version of your guilt after another.

II.   This may sound strange, but you must learn to accept Hell. Stop fighting it, hating it, hoping for salvation. Try to accept Hell without losing yourself. Practice self-love. Accept the frying pan on which you're being fried, and remember that the frying pan does not devalue all the good and worthy things you once had, and that no one can take those away from you.

III.   Refrain from telling yourself that you're doomed. Some people do leave Hell. We don't know how or why, but it does happen occasionally, that's certain. To start, you must stop desiring Hell while also being afraid of it. Because if you fear it and desire it at the same time— well, you know where that gets you. Quit working yourself up. You're in Hell already. We fear the unknown, but now that you're familiar with Hell, you know the devil is not nearly as bad as he is painted, so there's no longer any point in being afraid. If you believe in God, trust that there is no limit to His mercy and omnipotence, and that He can forgive and accept anyone, including you. Everyone has a chance at salvation.

IV.   You're free! Sure, you're in Hell, but that doesn't limit your freedom in any way; you're free to devote yourself to good or evil, to God or the devil. You're free, but at the same time you aren't in control of the situation, which is another thing you must accept. You can't stop being in Hell just because you want to. Don't expect sincere repentance to be followed by immediate deliverance, do not resort to bargaining and legal reasoning, stop gathering evidence to prove that you deserve something better than Hell. You must humbly come to terms with whatever happens.

V.   The main variety of torture here is fear. Therefore, develop a tolerance for your fear. Proceed from fear all the way to boredom. Let yourself get sick of being afraid, so that whatever scares you the most becomes less frightening than tedious. And don't look for consolation either. The worst has already happened. You must always go forward to meet your fear: not in order to fight it, but to accept it.

Many of my patients have departed Hell and write me letters from the higher realms, saying that therapy with me really helped them, but to be honest, I'm not sure that it was the therapy that did it. What did it, and how all of this really works, is honestly still completely baffling to me. In the meantime, I remain in Hell, and I don't know if this means that I'm doing something wrong, or that I have an important task to accomplish here, a rescue mission, or something along those lines. I just try to keep working, and the work distracts me a little from the flames, the sorrow, and the loneliness.

BIOMASS

There once was a teacher of literature, a highly spiritual lady, whose husband was an alcoholic. One day, her friend said to her, "I know this woman, a psychic. Go see her, maybe she can help." The literature teacher took her pitiful paycheck and went to visit the psychic. She told her, "This and that, my husband drinks, can you do something about it?"

The psychic looked at a photo of the husband and said: "Well, he doesn't have a soul."

"How's that?" asked the frightened literature teacher.

"No soul, that's how," said the psychic. "Biomass."

The literature teacher went home in low spirits. She tried to banish these thoughts about the soul. "What nonsense," she thought. "Everyone has a soul, so my husband must also have one. How could he be alive without a soul? It was his soul I fell in love with back then," she reasoned, "not his body all covered in hair, not his teeth going rotten." Be that as it may, the teacher kept trying to chase the thoughts away, but a worm of doubt persisted, and she remembered one thing, another, a third—how he let her down once, pulled some stunt another time, said something rude on a third occasion—and she saw that in all these situations there wasn't a whiff of soul. Sometimes she would come home from work and find her husband sprawled in front of the TV, drinking beer, or he'd snore drunkenly at night, or sit there scratching his balls without even taking the garbage out, and in those times she saw it clearly: Biomass. No soul. None.

Meanwhile, the husband noticed that his wife was always upset these days. He thought it was because of his drinking. And the wife's friend had told him about the wife going to see a psychic to get him to quit. He decided to have an honest conversation with her, set out his position, and put an end to her torment.

"Masha," he said to her, "sit down, let's talk." They sat. He looked her in the eye and said, "I drank, I drink, and I'm gonna keep drinking."

She was silent. He was also silent. Then she stood up and recited: "*There is no feeling in your eyes / there is no truth in your replies / and there's no soul within.*"

Unto the end be stalwart, heart, as the poem goes—so she left her husband. She couldn't go on living with a man whose soul was missing. All else being the same, but with a soul, she would have stayed somehow, endured it, but without a soul it was too much. The husband was immediately snapped up by the wife's friend, the one who'd recommended the psychic. She had already been his mistress for many years. But he went on drinking as usual, didn't see too big a difference. The friend then went to the same psychic and told her, "This and that, my man drinks, can you do something about it?"

The psychic looked at his photo and said: "Well, he doesn't have a soul. Biomass."

"Sure, but can you recommend something for the drinking?" asked the wife's friend.

The psychic gave her some herbs to put in his tea, and the friend went home satisfied. His having no soul—she didn't mind that too much. She had loved this man for many years; she loved him to death. And since she loved him to death, the lack of soul didn't really concern her. The wife's friend was a simple woman—she knew nothing of souls, but she loved bodies, particularly this man's.

So their days went, and then spring came. Buds bloomed in the trees, young leaves slipped forth, a fragrant web of flowers wove itself across the treetops. The literature teacher went to school and taught children the eternal spiritual truths that the great classic writers wrote about. Her soul yearned to rise. Soon, she met a man who shared her spiritual yearnings. He was the trainer of the fitness group she had joined. This man was a real guru, preaching the benefits of a healthy lifestyle and proper nutrition. The two of them moved in together, but before that, he asked her to get rid of her cat, because, he said, man should aspire upward, toward God, instead of cleaving to the lower forms of life. The teacher of literature gave the cat to her friend, the same one who now lived with her ex-husband. The friend fed the man and the cat, and made sure they were comfortable and cozy. Her soul did not yearn to rise, but flowed downward in a warm, dim stream, into material things, into matter, which she loved better than the Spirit. The man drank as before, lay sprawled in front of the TV, snored, scratched his balls, but, appreciating the good attitude of his new wife, did occasionally take the garbage out. The woman psychic bought herself a new apartment and car. In general, and on the whole, they were all happy and lived long, until one day they died, because happiness is achievable, but death is inevitable.

ACT OF NATURE

N was walking down the street one day, got to the intersection of Leninsky Prospekt and Zina Portnova Street, and saw something strange in the sky. At first, he thought it was a plane beginning to land—Pulkovo Airport was nearby. But then he looked closely and saw that it wasn't a plane at all, but a car flying through the air—pretty high up there, really small, but very clearly a car. N spat on the ground and decided it was a plane anyway.

The following evening N was walking down the street again, got to the intersection of Leninsky and Zina Portnova, and again saw something strange in the sky. He saw—can you just imagine—a car. As was his custom, N spat and decided it was a plane anyway. He walked a little farther down Leninsky, toward the Semya supermarket. But then he heard a peculiar sound, turned around, and saw a car falling from the sky to the ground. And crashing. All the other cars on the road started honking, and their drivers hopped out, pointing up at the sky. What a shitshow, thought N, and kept walking.

He stopped by the supermarket, came out with a little sack,

slowly headed back. But the intersection was now full of cops, ambulances, rescue vehicles. Traffic was at a standstill, and on the sidewalks people were running back and forth in a panic, looking up at the sky. In the sky cars appeared one after another, emerging from a dark void in the southwest, tracing an arc, and plummeting. Some of them crashed, turning into heaps of metal, while others for some reason landed very smoothly, as though on airbags, and drove off. But they didn't drive very far, because the cops and rescue services stopped them.

N went up to a cop on the sidewalk and asked him what was going on.

"What we have here," the cop said, "is cars falling from the sky, creating a public disturbance."

"But why," asked N, "aren't they all crashing?"

"Cause not yet established," said the cop. At that moment, two other cops brought over a young man who'd been behind the wheel of a car that just landed neatly on the pavement. "This," they reported, "is So-and-So, twenty-nine years old, his Volkswagen just landed, the license plate is such-and-such."

"What were you doing in the sky, what was your purpose in landing here?" asked the senior cop.

"I was just coming back from Tallinn," said the young man. "I spent the weekend there. And so I'm driving down the highway, it's dark, and then I look and see that all the other cars have apparently vanished and I'm driving through the sky, and so I drove like that for a little while, and then I sank lower and lower, and then I landed here. And down here," he gestured, "it's a real mess, and, anyway, you should let me get home to my mom."

All the other survivors said about the same thing. That night, over fifty cars fell from the sky—only eleven of them made it.

N came home feeling a little unwell on account of all this, but no big deal; he boiled some pelmeni, drank a glass of vodka, calmed himself down, and went online to see what other people were saying about it. On various internet forums people were arguing: some were writing things about UFOs, others about demons, a third group about a special new technology for the manufacture of flying cars, and a fourth group was claiming it was a false flag operation planned by special forces. At this point N registered for a forum and wrote: It was an act of nature.

HOME, TO MOLOGA

In '93, Vasily Gavrilovich Lastochkin turned seventy-six and went underwater. The water was where it had been for a long time now: five kilometers east of Svyatovsky Mokh Island, three kilometers north of the Babya Mountain fairway mark. He still remembered his town on the two rivers, the Mologa and the Volga, and right outside the town, the swamp and Svatoye Lake. In the old days, he had worked at the machine-tractor station and studied at the agricultural technical college. He was nineteen when they announced that the town of Mologa would be flooded by the reservoir. His grandfather, Karp, stayed behind.

"I'm old," he had said, "where am I going to go? I'll stay in the empty house. There's no life for me away from the fields I worked for years, away from the oak grove where your grandmother and I walked when we were young. But you and your mother ought to leave, save yourselves, go into the new life, into industrialization."

Vasily and his mother went to Leningrad, and there they lived; his mother died, he worked at the Kirov Factory until retirement. At the start of the '90s, the water level in the Rybinsk Reservoir went down, and part of the flooded town was exposed. In those fall days of early October, while Yeltsin warred with Parliament, Vasily Gavrilovich headed to the flooded town of his youth. He had recently buried his wife Nadya, his children were living their own lives, Yeltsin was not to Vasily Gavrilovich's liking, so he decided to go home, to Mologa. The old man brought with him photos of his children and grandchildren, and his favorite book, *Distant Rainbow*, by the Strugatsky brothers, and set out.

Vasily Gavrilovich bought a ticket for a train with the nice name Textilny Krai, terminating at Ivanovo, got off at the Nekouz station, and stuck out his arm—it was hitchhiking from here on out. The old man stood there, flagging down cars, until some skinheads stopped for him.

"Where ya headed, Gramps?"

"Home, to Mologa."

"The hell, where's that?"

"Toward Myshkin, then toward Vesyegonsk, through Borok, past the village of Vereteya, then before the village of Dubets you turn right and go through Dubrova toward Ostrogi. You can leave me there."

The skinheads took the old man in their car and drove him to where he'd said, the way it happens in fairy tales: *The bear will help you on your way, and the wolf, and the little humpbacked horse, and also a skinhead bandit.* The old man spent the night in Ostrogi, beneath an oak tree, then rose at dawn and continued on his way. He walked along the embankment of the old Mologa road, went down into the floodplain, turned left, crossed the Shumarovsky channel at its upper shallows, walked through the sand along the southern shore of Svyatovsky Mokh, over the flooded shoals, along the edge of a hummocky peat bog, and toward the northeast of the island—until he finally reached the outskirts of Mologa. And then Vasily Gavrilovich Lastochkin saw the town's cobbled streets, its wrought iron grates, the gravestones in its cemetery. An enormous, whiskered, golden-brown carp swam up to him. And the flooded Mologa flowed like milk.

A RUSSIAN PROPHET

The Prophets Isaiah and Ezekiel dined with me . . .
—Blake, *The Marriage of Heaven and Hell*

The Truth began when the cat brought us fire.

Thus began Pavel Nesterov's book. The poet Pavel Nesterov wrote high-minded poems and believed that they were the real deal. But he also wanted to make money, so he wrote a book of Russian esoterica called *The Truth of the Slavs*. He'd read about the cat in a VKontakte group called Everyday Philosophy. The cat featured in a fairy tale: *Atop the craggiest crag, the highest height, the billy goat and the ram wanted to build a fire, so the cat wove birchbark around the billy goat's horns and told the billy goat and the ram to knock their heads together. Sparks shot from their eyes, and the bark ignited.* Pavel Nesterov located this event as the origin of the Truth of the Slavs.

He found all of his other material on VKontakte too, in various groups—Transcendental Meditation for Tradwives, Curing Erectile Dysfunction with Kundalini Yoga—and to make it all look legitimate, he wrote that the prophets Isaiah, Ezekiel, Daniel, and Jonah also spoke of these things, and that anyone who didn't believe him could go look it up in the Bible. And, anyway, the Bible had really been written by Slavs, and the biblical YHWH was actually the Slavic deity Rod. Pavel Nesterov chuckled a lot to himself as he wrote, so the text came out spirited and moving.

He thought he'd rake in piles of money, but what happened far outpaced his expectations: his book inspired a new religious movement, with adherents who called themselves the Nesterovians. The Nesterovians considered Pavel Nesterov to be a Russian prophet in the line of Isaiah, Ezekiel, Daniel, and Jonah. Every day, Pavel Nesterov received letters from people who wrote that he'd opened their eyes and changed their lives, that his book had become their new Bible, that they were now proud of their homeland and its spiritual traditions, that they'd always felt, deep down, that things were the way he'd said they were . . . A few people even self-immolated because of his book. Pavel Nesterov got a little spooked.

"But it's a fake, an obvious fake, why are people taking it so seriously?" Pavel wondered. "And why doesn't anyone care about my poems, they're the real deal!" Pavel had this thought and then suddenly realized that it was all one and the same. His poems, which he'd taken seriously, were fakes, too. He'd written them the same way he wrote his book about the Slavs, not really knowing what he was writing about, and he'd considered his ignorance a gift from God. But now he saw that the same creative process was at work both in the "fake" scripture and the "authentic" poetry. It was only that the poems were a more sophisticated fake, a loftier one—which is why nobody cared about them at all. Or maybe everyone had seen from the start that the poems were fake, because all poems are fake, but the book about the Slavs pretended to have a claim to the truth, and though this claim had only been a game for him, people had bought it. Both the poems and the book were, and at the same time were not, fraudulent. And then something shifted in Pavel Nesterov's mind, and he could no longer distinguish between what was real and what wasn't. In this way things had once shifted in the minds of all the prophets.

And Pavel Nesterov began to believe everything he himself had written, and he set out on a journey across Russia to search for the prophets Isaiah, Ezekiel, Daniel, and Jonah, to ask them whether he had understood everything correctly, and whether it was true that he was also a prophet now, as the Nesterovians claimed. He walked and walked, deep into the country, into the dark night, into the depths of the past, the centuries rewinding around him like a film strip, then the frames ran out and there was only emptiness, and from the earth arose four earthen old men: Ivashko Sosuyi, Kharlo Ivashkov, Polezhai Skoromokh, and Palka Andronov. And Pavel Nesterov asked them: "Are you prophets?" And the old men said, in English, "Yes."

"O, Russian prophets," prayed Pavel Nesterov, "reveal the truth to me, what does it mean to be a prophet? Have you seen God? Have you heard His voice?"

Ivashko Sosuyi said, *"I saw no God, nor heard any, but I was persuaded that the voice of honest indignation is the Voice of God."*

Then Pavel Nesterov asked, *"Does a firm persuasion that a thing is so, make it so?"*

And the old men said, "Yes, if you can believe."

And Kharlo Ivashkov said, *" We of Israel taught that the Poetic Genius was the first principle, and all the others merely derivative.* Such is the God of Israel."

And the old men said, "Would you be present at the birth of Poetic Genius? You must pass us and journey farther, deeper, into the very heart of the empty earth."

And Pavel Nesterov went deeper into the country and its emptiness, and he saw the craggiest crag, the highest height, and the billy goat, the ram, and the cat. And the cat brought about fire, and that fire was Poetic Genius, the origin of all things. It was the Alpha and the Omega. Pavel Nesterov then saw a house somewhere in Serbia, and he went inside, and the master of the house said to him, "I'm going to riddle you three riddles, and you must tell me the answers to all three." Pavel Nesterov looked and saw the master of the house pointing toward the fire in the fireplace, the cat on the bench, and the attic. And Pavel saw that the cat was the very same one who had brought about fire, and the fire in the fireplace wasn't simply fire but Poetic Genius, and the attic was not an attic but the Palace of Wisdom.

"That's easy," said Pavel Nesterov, "that over there is He who brought us fire, Poetic Genius, and the Palace of Wisdom."

"You're a moron," said his host, "that's a cat, a fire in the fireplace, and the attic."

That night, Pavel Nesterov took the cat, tied a tinder stick to its tail, and used the fire in the fireplace to set the stick alight, and the cat ran up to the attic, starting a housefire.

"Hey, boss, get up, or keep sleeping, doesn't matter now, you're the moron," Pavel Nesterov called. "He who brought us fire has seized the flame of Poetic Genius and carried it into the Palace of Wisdom! I, the prophet Pavel Nesterov, with the help of Poetic Genius, now incinerate the Palace of Wisdom, and join the prophets' eternal throng! Here, at the meeting of Alpha and Omega, I write my new book, ablaze with flame, since it is said—"

The Truth came to an end when the cat spread the fire and burned down the house.

MISHENKA THE CONTRARIAN

A Tale of Doves and Evil

He denied everything, including the location of the earth below and the sky above. A happy man, Mishenka the Contrarian. He was the most wicked and disobedient boy in his class, back at the end of the '40s. He did everything backward, out of spite, and his teacher nicknamed him accordingly: Mishenka the Contrarian. He'd understood early on that things did not work the way adults said they did. His mother would tell him that it's not good to litter, and in his own mind Mishenka would flip "not good" to "good" and litter with delight. When he saw someone else littering, he was happy, too. When he saw someone crying, he was glad. When he saw someone hurting the weak, he was overjoyed. After all, if things like that don't make you happy, life can be painful—so unbearably painful—there's so much violence and injustice and hunger and death everywhere—and Mishenka didn't want to be in pain, so he swapped things around in his head.

He'd been doing this since he was a little boy, when he saw a German soldier in the occupied village of Obukhovka, and right before his eyes the soldier struck Mishenka's father. Mishenka had felt several things at once, then—horror, outrage, hate; these things were suffocating him, and he burst out laughing. Soon after, he figured out that the minute he heard some inner voice—his mother's voice, or the voice of human morality, entering into a child's soul—telling him that something wasn't good, he could immediately summon another voice, mighty and superhuman, probably belonging to that very same German soldier, and that voice would laugh and tell him, "Rejoice!"

And that's how Mishenka the Contrarian reeducated himself and learned to see as good everything that people usually understood as evil, and everything that people understood as evil he saw the other way, as good. All his life, he rejoiced at deaths, misfortunes, and the blows of fate, and he grew despondent in those rare moments when something compelled him to tenderness and pity, or when he came across something beautiful or listened to music. He knew that the obverse of beauty and music were pain, loss, and doom, so he couldn't be happy with these, like other people. He fell in love with a young woman once, but he told her, "You're going to get old and ugly anyway, and then you'll die," and left her. While he had loved her, he'd felt a dull, unremitting, animal ache, but when he left her, he felt better.

Mishenka the Contrarian thought that he'd outsmarted life, which so amply produced causes for suffering and scattered them beneath people's feet like acorns from an oak tree, while he, in the alchemical vessel of his soul, had transformed all the acorns of suffering into the gold of gladness, and because of this he was happier than other people. A nasty old man, at this very moment he's hanging out of his bedroom window with a slingshot, shooting at pigeons and cursing toothlessly. He aims at the most beautiful white dove and his aim is true.

THE CHILDREN OF THE CITY OF NOVOSTRADOV

—black cloths and organs, —lightning and thunder, —rise and roll; —Waters and sorrows, rise and revive the Floods. For since they subsided, — oh . . . so boring!

—Rimbaud, tr. John Ashbery, "After the Flood"

In the '90s, all the children in the city of Novostradov were sure that on New Year's Eve in the year 2000, Ahura Mazda and Ahriman would appear in the sky and a great war would begin. The children would fight on opposing sides in this war, some for the Dark and others for the Light. After the war, the world as they knew it would end, and planet Earth would merge with its double, the planet Nibiru, which was already drawing closer. If Earth was a haven for technological innovation, Nibiru was home to a highly developed system of magic, and it was populated by elves, dragons, and gnomes. When Earth and Nibiru became one, magic and technology would also merge, and in the new world harmony would reign.

All the children of Novostradov were also convinced that they had magical powers. Preschoolers in apartment courtyards told each other about Ahura Mazda and Ahriman, the coming war, the merging of the planets, and the fact that they were, all of them, wielders of magic. Kids knew all this since their sandbox days, but it was considered necessary to keep the knowledge secret from adults. Every child believed that they were assisted by several invisible spirits, and every child knew which side they'd be on when the war came, Light or Dark. Kids associated with others of their kind and disliked members of the opposition. If a boy developed a crush on a girl, the first thing he had to find out was whether she was Light or Dark. Sometimes it happened that love brought a child over to the opposing side, and this introduced genuine drama to the children's lives.

In every other regard, the children of Novostradov did not differ significantly from other children in other cities. They were likewise interested in gum, Snickers, new jeans, cartoons, and Dendy and Sega video games.

On New Year's Eve, as the year changed to 2000, kids from preschoolers to high school seniors gathered in the streets, waiting for the coming of Ahura Mazda and Ahriman. Lovingly bundled by their mothers in winter scarves, prepared to battle to the death for their god, crowds of children stood and stared expectantly into the sky. A wet snow was falling, grown-ups were uncorking bottles of champagne and setting off fireworks, but Ahura Mazda and Ahriman did not make an appearance.

For another year or so, the children waited: maybe the war would begin after all, and the planet Nibiru, with its elves and gnomes, would approach the Earth. But the war did not begin, and Nibiru did not come near, either. Out of inertia, many children still continued to wait, but some were already beginning to sneer at the idea of Ahura Mazda and Ahriman, and many others simply avoided the subject, as though nothing like that had ever come up. The children were less and less interested in who'd been Dark and who'd been Light, they no longer really mentioned their magical powers, and life now seemed to consist of nothing more than gum, Snickers, jeans, cartoons, and video games.

The kids who had been very young in the year 2000 soon forgot completely about the war, Ahura Mazda and Ahriman, the planet Nibiru, and that New Year's night. In their minds, all those stories became mixed up with other fairy tales they heard from their parents as children. It was harder for the teens. Some of them started drinking, others got into drugs; the girls buzzed their heads and went hitchhiking around the country. But as time passed, many went back to school, found jobs, started families, had children, divorced. They bought cell phones, made social media accounts. And soon, very soon thereafter, Novostradov no longer differed in any way from other provincial Russian towns with high rates of alcoholism and unemployment.

DELUSIONS OF BEING

Intoxicating joy and self-forgetting, did the world once seem to me.
—Nietzsche, tr. Thomas Common

On spring evenings, with the scent of bird cherry and a verdant coolness in the air, and little skeletons of flowers raining down upon the sidewalks, math teacher Hektor Aristarkhovich was beset by delusions of being. This was connected in some way to the soul, to sorrow, and to fate, but it was more transparent than all of these, and purer, thought Hektor Aristarkhovich.

It was purer because every person had a particular soul, sorrow, and fate, and these gave rise to individual delusions, which people usually spent their entire lives believing, never quite seeing through them, but only dreaming some pointless, ridiculous dream, a drag, a bore—although maybe one did come to one's senses occasionally, sometimes, at night, like a corpse rising from its coffin to malign the heavens. But delusions *of being* weren't the same as human delusions, which were the consequences of indigestion, the build-up of sperm, or the uptake of dopamine and serotonin. These delusions were the delusions *of being itself*. As an evil-smelling swamp emits miasmic fumes, as the sea swells into the waves of the tide that crash against the shore, so *being creates its own delusions*, and these delusions, like the waves of the sea, wash over people on spring evenings such as these, transparent as clear alcoholic spirits (while people's personal delusions are the diluted version).

Whenever delusions of being set upon Hektor Aristarkhovich, he would begin to suffer, and leave his home to wander the neighborhood and observe the bums, the lovers, the tailless cats, the obscene greenery breaking furiously through death—and within it, our foremothers and forefathers reproaching the living and yearning for them. And he heard the call of love in the songs of courting birds, and he saw how hopelessly damaged and hideous people were, as though each one bore a mortal wound. Hektor Aristarkhovich would wish to be rid of these delusions of being, and head out to buy some beer and get drunk and dumb, but the beer also contained within it the delusions of being, it was live beer, and some guy trailed after Hektor Aristarkhovich as he left the shop, yelling, "Just give me a sip, my belly's all dried up, I'm John Barleycorn."

And from beneath the earth, beneath the squelching mud and the teeming grass, heads arose, heads bereft of bodies, and gave themselves peculiar names: "I'm Priest Mush-for-Brains; I'm Bob for Stew; I'm Bean Goose." And everything in the world, Hektor Aristarkhovich saw, was madness and desperation, all of it perjurious and sacrilegious. Some women walked by, wind-swept, penetrable, but grinning evilly, like witches. The viburnum bush was a wandering bard, the rowan tree was a redheaded wench, the neighbor was taking her son, who had Down syndrome, out for a walk, and the kids playing in the sandbox were raving. The delusions of being rose and streamed forth like a river at high tide, flooding fields and orchards. The moon rose and spilled milk into this flooded kingdom of delusion. Hector Aristarkhovich walked and wept, because everything around him was doomed, unsalvageable, mortal, and he himself was a finished man, and he saw two naked women: one had tied the other to a birch tree and was whipping her ass with fresh nettles.

And Hektor Aristarkhovich wished for someone to tie him to a birch too, and whip his naked ass; he wanted to be stung by bees, wasps, and hornets in this unholy paradise between highrises on the outskirts of the city, where radiant, lamenting spirits holding candles danced in circles around him. They were laying him to rest, he understood, they were holding a funeral service with candles in their hands, like a matins service. He lay in the sandbox, and the sandbox was an open grave. Butterflies fluttered around Hektor Aristarkhovich, candles burned, the spirits cried and called out: You idiot Hektor Aristarkhovich, you moron Hektor Aristarkhovich, you piece of shit Hektor Aristarkhovich. Grasshoppers and mole crickets chirped, mushrooms grew from the walls of the old apartment blocks, and an ant dragged its larvae into Hektor Aristarkhovich's mouth, but the ant was enormous, big as a hand, and what it dragged into Hektor Aristarkhovich's mouth wasn't larvae but a slippery white member. A rain of tears was falling, with pollen and a fine dusting of nectar dissolved in its drops . . . The crazed tears of the earth, her sweet face, hailing the heavenly city, emerald and amethyst hail, minute particles of ice suddenly landing her a thousand slaps. And frantic, lunatic music filling his ears: the demented birds' choir of this lustful paradise, their gurgling, and chirping, and chirring, and the haunted melody of the nightingale. And at dawn, when the distinction between comedy and tragedy is erased, the world didn't appear to Hektor Aristarkhovich to be the dream of a god, no, but rather an intricate, transparent pang of love, sprung from the firm foundation of desire and death, a spontaneous delirium without creator or cure, a seething byproduct of madness—or so it seemed to him on those quiet mornings when the delusions subsided and he went to school to teach children math.

THE CASE OF SHCHAVELIEV

The whole terrible ordeal in the life of bank clerk Veniamin Shchaveliev began when he turned forty-five and went to renew his passport. At the passport office there was a woman with a deep scowl and a purple chemical perm—as Veniamin remembered later, once he returned home. He also remembered one other thing—after he'd signed his new passport, the woman had handed him another document, which he also signed, more or less automatically. But what that other document was, Veniamin could not remember. A vague disquiet arose in his soul.

What could it have been? Veniamin wondered. He stopped sleeping, stopped eating, and finally went back to the passport office. "What did I sign here? What kind of document did you give me?" he asked the woman with the scowl and the purple perm. The woman just shrugged, saying, "You didn't sign anything else here, you just signed your new passport, you're imagining things." Veniamin brought his fist down on the table: "Tell me, you hag, what kind of document did you slip me?!" The woman shouted that he was insane and chased him from the office.

Veniamin came home and began trying hard to remember, as he was always doing now, what the document had actually been. "Seems like . . . seems like . . ." he muttered to himself, crinkling his forehead—"it was a loan! Of course! It was an enormous loan!" He called all the banks in the city, but no bank could confirm that it had approved him for a loan. And then Veniamin realized, or thought he did, that it was even worse: the document wasn't paperwork for a loan, it was the deed to his apartment! This new-found clarity even calmed Veniamin down, briefly, and then he set out to take decisive action. He went to the Frunzenskaya District police station, told the cops about the mysterious document, and asked: "May I write a statement saying that I was tricked into providing my signature and this deed to my apartment is not valid?" The cops were at a loss, but Veniamin was so anxious, and his hands were shaking so badly, that they decided to let him make his statement. He wrote it down and headed home with a sense of absolute relief.

At home Veniamin lay down on the couch, in need of a break, turned on the TV, and saw the Patriarch and Putin. He looked absentmindedly at the Patriarch's vestments, the gold, the beard. And then a thought, horrible and frightening, flashed through his mind like dark lightning. He had finally remembered. The document hadn't been a loan or even a deed, no. It was a contract with the Devil regarding the sale of his soul. Veniamin dashed around his apartment, howling and tearing out his hair. He had never been a religious man, but now he understood that it was all real: eternal bliss and eternal damnation, God and Satan, and the jolly flames of Hell.

Veniamin stopped going to work, stopped washing and shaving. He wrote a letter to Patriarch Kirill, the Head of the Russian

Orthodox Church, saying that he'd made a deal with the Devil, and was kindly requesting that the Patriarch, using his holy powers, declare the agreement void. For a long time there was no answer to his letter, but one day Veniamin turned on the TV again and saw that the Patriarch was giving a speech. Then he turned suddenly toward Veniamin, looked him right in the eye, and said, "Your deal can't be declared void. I've made one just like it." Then Veniamin wrote a letter to Putin, obsequious and abject: "I beseech you as our dear Father, our Batman, Transformer, Spiderman Putin, the Crimea is definitely ours, united with Russia through your might and strength, so with your powers of the highest Nietzschean Superman Buddha and Zarathustra over America and Obama, command the Devil to annul his deal with me so that there is no nuclear war." Putin likewise responded through the TV. "Oh, brother Venya, you can't get out of that deal, I have one too, so do all our people. And I've decreed that from this year forward all citizens must sign this deal when they renew their passports, it's a kind of reform we've passed, there's a bill about it, it's crucial for the stability of the country. Or the American bastards will conquer us."

So what was left for Veniamin to do? He had one more idea, a pretty decent one, thinking back to how he'd gotten out of army service: I'll pretend to be crazy, he thought, my signature can't be considered valid, not if I'm declared insane. He called an ambulance and told them, "I'm delirious and hallucinating, it's acute paranoid schizophrenia, Kandinsky-Clérambault Syndrome, come right away, I haven't gone to work in six months, I've been writing letters to Putin and the Patriarch and they're talking to me through the TV." That was how he played it. He was declared insane, institutionalized, and prescribed a bunch of pills. He was no longer fit for society. Not fit for society, sure—and maybe not fit for the Devil either, Veniamin thought slyly. All things considered, living out your life in an asylum for the mentally ill is a small price to pay for getting out of burning in the flames of Hell for all eternity.

On his first night at the asylum, which was the thirtieth of January, Veniamin had a dream. In the dream, he's walking down a road through the fields of some distant country, and coming toward him is an old man with a weathered face, dressed in simple clothing. "What troubles you, son?" the man asks in an unknown tongue, but Veniamin understands everything he says. "I'm troubled, Father, because I've made a deal with the Devil. But who are you?" "I'm Granddad Vasily. Let us pray together about your misfortune." Granddad Vasily takes Veniamin by the hand, and they begin to pray together: "King of Kings and Lord of Lords, creator of the fiery ranks . . ." They pray, and then Granddad Vasily says, "Could this, son, be the paper you lost?" and takes out a sheet of paper. Veniamin looks and recognizes it: yes, it's the very same one that he signed back there at the passport office, as though in a trance; he couldn't remember what it looked like before, but here it is now, with the words *I, Veniamin Shchaveliev, sell my soul to our Master the Devil*, and here's the seal of Hell, and the number 666, and his signature at the bottom is melting away before his very eyes, disappearing, now it's completely gone . . .

TABOO

The art critic N was always on Facebook posting about something highly intellectual. He knew that he could say anything, with three exceptions, but these three exceptions were precisely the things that concerned him the most; they were the things he burned to share. The three things he so wanted to post on Facebook were: "I came home drunk as shit again;" "I want to fuck;" and "Help me find a job." Stupid thoughts always lodge in your mind, and so he was sorely tempted to write these things, particularly the first one, but he held back, so as not to tarnish his reputation. However, once he came home drunk as shit, as was his custom, and couldn't help himself. He pulled up Facebook and typed: "So I came home drunk as shit again. And I want to fuck. And I need a job. That's all." After that he went to bed and dozed drunkenly through the night. In the morning he woke with a sense of having done something irrevocable. He opened Facebook—and what do you know, nothing bad had happened. Waiting for him there were forty likes, one invitation to fuck, and not one single job offer. Then he posted some high-minded reflections about the influence of the avant-garde on a certain contemporary artist.

VENUS

For some time now, H has been persecuted by Venus.

It all started when he began keeping a journal. He wrote in it for a week or two, then read over what he'd written. Either there was nothing at all going on in H's life or his inner world, or whatever was going on was so appalling that H couldn't bear to record it—but practically the sole content of each day's entry was an encounter with Venus.

For instance: one day H went to the Borey Art Center—so he wrote in his journal—and got drunk there with some writers, which was reasonable enough. Then he went out onto Nevsky Prospekt, stood there, swaying a bit, and tried to light a cigarette—but Venus up in the sky was blinding him. And not just Venus, but an enormous full moon. And also Mars; Mars had just come nearer to Earth. The worst, however, was Venus. H tried to get away, and rode the trolleybus for a long time, but Venus followed him.

Another time, H went to the movies with a friend; as he left the theater, Venus was there in the sky again, blinding him. And an enormous full moon, bathed in yellow glow. The moon wasn't so bad, but Venus . . .

Or how about this: H was visiting some friends living off the Politekhnicheskaya metro stop; they split a bottle of Jewish Standard vodka and went to stroll around the Benois Garden. They thought it would be very glamorous: nighttime, being drunk, the Benois Garden. But the garden was an open expanse covered in ice and shit, where H's feet got soaked while he tried to break into the ruins of a burned-out farm. Nearby loomed the white, Mordor-esque, technocratic tower of the State Scientific Center for Robotics and Technical Cybernetics. None of this seemed particularly ominous—but then suddenly, without warning, bright and shameless, mind-shattering, like a round of gunfire . . . Venus.

Or this one. H went to an analytic philosophy seminar on Kripke where someone was giving a lecture H didn't understand at all, except for the words "Hesperus" and "Phosphorus," meaning that the lecture was about Venus. After the seminar, H went outside and saw what he saw in the sky. You know what he saw. He didn't try to run, just walked to the bus stop, thinking, "Why do we suppose that Hesperus and Lucifer, the morning star and the evening star, are one and the same? We probably think they're the same because we're referencing an object, the actual planet Venus. But if one allows that Hesperus is something other than Lucifer, then other, more complex propositions arise, there's no longer a reference, no assumption of the inviolability of the world. Lucifer and Hesperus, Hesperus and Lucifer . . ."

So H went on muttering to himself. Then he came home and burned his journal.

TERENTIY'S GUILT

In the evenings, the accountant Terentiy had conversations with his feelings of guilt. Terentiy's guilt asked him various questions.

"Are you guilty of being late to work?" Terentiy's guilt would ask him. Terentiy, straining to remember, would discover that no, he had come to work precisely at ten.

"Not guilty!" Terentiy would happily reply.

"Let's see," the guilt would scowl. "Are you guilty of coming to work on time?"

"Yes, I'm guilty," Terentiy would mournfully admit.

"Are you guilty of being rude to your boss?" questioned his guilt.

"No, certainly not," Terentiy would say, alarmed.

"Then perhaps you're guilty of being polite to your boss?" the guilt pressed him.

"I am guilty, yes," Terentiy would mournfully admit.

"Are you guilty of making a mistake in the accounts?"

"No, that's impossible, so help me God!" Terentiy would swear.

"Are you then guilty of doing the accounts correctly?"

"Lord Almighty, I am guilty of that, definitely guilty," Terentiy would woefully confess.

Crushed by his feelings of guilt, he went to bed and dreamed bad dreams, woke with his alarm in the morning, arrived at work in a timely fashion, spoke courteously to the woman who was his boss, and calculated the accounts without a single error. At home, stationed on the couch, his guilt was waiting for him. It seemed to expect something different from him—but what that was, Terentiy did not know.

INCIDENTAL PLEASURES

Vasily lives through incidental pleasures. Not even really *lives*—more like survives. Say he's heading home on the metro, and he thinks to himself, "I'll get home, and then I'll kill myself." But he's really hungry, so he goes to a café and eats some junk there, starts feeling pleasantly relaxed and too lazy to kill himself, and moves the whole thing to tomorrow. Then Vasily remembers that tomorrow X is coming over and they're going to have amazing sex, and he postpones suicide to the day after that.

And so it drags on: incidental pleasures and delayed execution. Each new pleasure is a reason to defer. This helps Vasily to fool death and to fool himself, and to wait, in secret, for one fine day when meaning will come into his life again, not the same kind of meaning that had been there earlier at some point, before it was lost, but an even better meaning, a new one, which will have in it something of all the meanings and all the aims that he has ever had, and will also contain something else, something that had never been there previously, and then Vasily will really live—but in the meantime, all the world's pleasures, all its small joys, will sustain him: bistros and coffee shops, cheesecake and Coca-Cola, gripping books and fun TV shows, bars and movie theaters, and time with friends, and attractive women, and sweet cats, springtime parks, warm baths, good tobacco.

All these things seem to call out to him: "Live, Vasily! Although we can't provide you with anything greater than ourselves, we also won't leave you! We'll stand between you and death until you find something better than us."

Nothing better has thus far been found. Vasily eats well, sleeps soundly, goes to the movies, sees friends, takes walks around the city.

ETERNAL SEPARATION

Arkadiy Lvovich, a quiet, kind, utterly reliable person, sits on the couch with his cat Barsik and watches TV. Barsik is grooming himself, paying no attention to Arkadiy Lvovich.

Today, Arkadiy Lvovich saw his ex-wife Dasha. He looked into her eyes and her still-beautiful face and remembered that when he and Dasha were young, they helped each other to comprehend the various mysteries of the universe. Most of these mysteries had turned out to be absolutely awful.

One of the most awful mysteries was the mystery of eternal separation, which had agonized Arkadiy Lvovich on an intuitive level ever since he was a child, but became even more significant later on. Arkadiy Lvovich thought back to his final summer with Dasha. Their relationship had been on the rocks for a long time, five years or so, and Dasha had already told him that she'd met someone else and was leaving him. At that point, Dasha worked at an office, and he didn't work anywhere. And so she called him every day to ask him to meet her during her lunch break, and he would go, and together they would walk to a cafeteria and have lunch. But for what? Why did Dasha keep calling him? Why did he keep going? Arkadiy Lvovich understood: it was so they could be together in the face of eternal separation.

Ever since then, Arkadiy Lvovich saw eternal separation looming on the horizon of any relationship, any time spent with other people. Arkadiy Lvovich tried not to turn anyone down for any reason. He thought that if even people stayed together until their deaths, as he and Dasha once hoped to do, it was all a tiny speck compared to eternal separation: years, centuries, millennia, frozen stretches of cosmos in which these people wouldn't exist and no trace of them would remain. And he valued every sort of human closeness probably precisely because of eternal separation. Sometimes Arkadiy Lvovich's mother, or a friend of his, or some woman, would say, "Come sit with me," "Let's chat," or "Join me for tea," and Arkadiy Lvovich would say no, and then be struck by the feeling that that eternal separation was imminent, and here he was turning people down. So Arkadiy Lvovich never argued and always tried to smooth things over. How could people go to war and kill one another, hurt each other, do all kinds of harm? It seemed to him that all this happened only because humanity hadn't grasped the concept of eternal separation.

He was so tormented by this premonition of eternal separation that in order to overcome it he was prepared to believe in God, if only God could guarantee that he, Arkadiy Lvovich, would be reunited with everyone he loved, if not on Earth, then in heaven: his departed father, his beloved childhood German shepherd Steffi, his ex-wife Dasha, the girls he had crushes on in school, old friends who had long gone their separate ways. Even between himself and his mother, an elderly woman who lived in the next room, Arkadiy Lvovich felt an eternal separation. She seemed to be by his side, and Arkadiy Lvovich did love her, but he remembered that as a small child he had loved her differently. He remembered how young and beautiful she had been, how happy he was to be with her—just as happy as he'd been with Dasha when he was in love. But now his mother was simply a dear, close, familiar person, and the oneness he'd felt with her when he a child was gone. When Arkadiy Lvovich grew up and lost that oneness it was like he'd lost his mother. And though they lived together and loved each other, they were already eternally separated, and nothing in the world could change that.

Arkadiy Lvovich, a quiet, kind, utterly reliable person, sits on the couch with his cat Barsik and watches TV. Barsik is grooming himself, paying no attention to Arkadiy Lvovich. Arkadiy Lvovich sits at one end of the couch, Barsik at the other, and eternal separation stretches between them.

PETROVICH
AND PETROVSKY

Petrovich the bum sat at a bus stop, brooding: everything in his life had gone wrong. Then a foreign car pulled up, and from the car emerged—here Petrovich did a double take—his spitting image, only this guy was dressed in a suit and seemed pretty cocky. He headed right for Petrovich and introduced himself: "I'm Petrovsky the oligarch. For a long time now I've been looking for someone who looks just like me. Recently my boys spotted you picking through expired sausages and refrigerator parts at the local dump, and they tipped me off. So I've come here to meet you, brother."

"What do you need me for, brother?" asked Petrovich the bum. "I'm a bum, you're an oligarch, I'm up to my ears in shit and you're up to yours in chocolate, what do we have in common but our ugly mugs?"

"I'm depressed," said Petrovsky the oligarch. "Everything in my life has gone wrong. Every billion that lands in my lap on the regular brings me only despair; I have so many model girlfriends I can't even get it up anymore; I've tried tricyclic antidepressants,

SSRIs, MAOIs, I even fooled around with herbal remedies, but nothing helps, brother. So I've decided to disappear, switch places with someone who looks just like me, and live that person's life, stop being an oligarch and just be happy. You, brother, can go be the oligarch instead of me."

Petrovich the bum was no fool, so he agreed. The oligarch became a bum, and the bum became an oligarch. Only something didn't quite work about their arrangement.

"I thought my life was shit, but it turns out an oligarch's life is even shittier," Petrovich the bum soon realized. "I'm so sick of business, sick of the girlfriends, sick of my competitors, and everybody hates me. I can be lounging somewhere on the Canary Islands with a blonde model in my lap, and all I can think is—wouldn't it be nice right now to sit out in the sunshine by some garbage bins, down a little vodka, catcall the girls walking by, pick fleas from my beard . . . Wasn't that happiness?"

Meanwhile, Petrovsky the oligarch, who had become a bum, also couldn't hack it: he wasn't up to drinking all day, the fleas in his beard annoyed him, attics were too cold to sleep in, and somehow life without business deals turned out to be a bit boring. He began reminiscing—the international airports, the hotels, the meetings, the receptions—and thinking: Wasn't that happiness?

Anyway, three years went by. Petrovich the bum drank his way through all the oligarch's money, bankrupted his company, and became a bum again. He picked fleas from his beard, warmed himself in the sun, sucked down vodka, and was happy. Petrovsky the oligarch built himself up from nothing over those years, founded a new company, started taking meetings again, flying into international airports, and getting it up perfectly well for his model girlfriends. And until they died a year later, when Petrovich the bum froze to death, drunk in a ditch, and Petrovsky the oligarch was shot by a hitman hired by one of his competitors, they were both grateful for everything they had, and understood that everything in their lives was going just fine. You just have to look at it from a different perspective—a different perspective, brother.

POLYAMORY

Lena, who was genderqueer, went to see a gynecologist because of an itch. "We'll have to test for sexually transmitted infections," said the gynecologist, Kozkina.

"I always use condoms," said Lena, "there's no way I could have caught something."

"You should get tested anyway," said Kozkina. "Chlamydia, for instance, can pass through tears in a condom. Do you have a single sexual partner?"

"No," said Lena, and grew pale, imagining terrible chlamydias gnawing through latex with their teeth.

"You poor girl," said Kozkina, "now you have to worry about chlamydia, when the best thing would be just to have a single sexual partner and to trust that person."

Lena couldn't stand it any longer, and said, "You're the poor woman—I'm not a girl, I'm genderqueer. And I don't think the best thing is having a single sexual partner. I'm polyamorous. Do you know what means? *Polyamory is the ethical practice of having intimate relationships with more than one partner, with the informed consent of all partners involved, on the basis of honesty, trust, and openness.* And I think polyamory is much better than mechanical serial monogamy with all the cheating and the lies."

"Is that like free love?" asked Kozkina.

"No, free love deteriorated a long time ago into having sex with just anyone, while polyamory is about long-term, ethical relationships," said Lena.

This conversation gave the gynecologist Kozkina something to ponder. "Polyamory, what a word," she thought to herself, leaving the clinic. Walking down the wide avenue toward the metro, she occasionally passed cafés with little tables outside and couples sitting at the tables, and walking past her there were other couples and singles, men and women, and the gynecologist Kozkina looked at them and wondered: Could you really love all these people and have relationships with them all? Kozkina imagined that people were all connected to one another by complicated, multi-faceted bonds of love, while she herself wasn't connected to anyone by such bonds, because for eighteen years now her only partner had been her husband, and all she saw in all her days were her husband and women's genitals. What a strange, foreign, mysterious country was Polyamory. It wasn't given to a simple Soviet person to understand.

A week later, Lena came back for test results. The tests didn't show any hidden infections, just a regular bacterial imbalance. But the gynecologist Kozkina soon got gonorrhea, because she trusted her husband and didn't use protection, but he had something going on the side, and not for the first time, either. And gynecologist Kozkina wondered whether she should get a divorce, but in the end she forgave her husband, since love suffers long, and is kind, endures all things, and never fails.

OY OY OY

There's a man lying down in a grave somewhere
With the same tattoos as me.

        —Coil

In the bathroom of the Krasnoyarsk airport, pop starlet Amanda, passing through on her tour, happened to glance at the cleaning schedule and froze: the cleaning woman's signature was precisely the same as Amanda's own signature. Every crook, every curl—it was all identical, as though Amanda herself had signed it. Amanda couldn't understand how such a thing was possible, and that very same day she hired a private investigator to dig up every detail about this cleaning woman. The following morning, the investigator told Amanda that the cleaner's name was Lyudmila Pashkevich; she was forty-four years old, uneducated, living in workers' housing in the Sovetsky neighborhood of Krasnoyarsk, and there was nothing special about her. Plus, on top of all that, she had a harelip. Amanda had just about calmed down when the investigator produced copies of all of the cleaning woman's official documents, including a job application she had written out by hand, and to her horror, Amanda saw that Lyudmila Pashkevich's handwriting was precisely the same as her own.

All this made Amanda very apprehensive. Like a thorn in her

heel, the cleaning woman tormented her. After all, she had been doing just fine, recording music, visiting her cosmetologist and her tanning salon, dating her boyfriend, and knowing no woes— but now there was Pashkevich.

Amanda tried to put the woman out of her mind. "No, no, I have nothing in common with her, who cares about a signature, who cares about someone's handwriting? It's just a coincidence, it happens," she told herself. Her concert went well, though she didn't perform her newest song. Not a soul in the world had heard it yet; Amanda had written it only recently and intended to return to Moscow and record it in the studio. The song went like this: "I love you and you love me / we're together finally / you're my joy / oy oy oy!" Amanda was going to dedicate the song to her boyfriend.

Waiting for her return flight after the concert, Amanda decided to step into the airport bathroom. "You don't scare me, Pashkevich," she thought, though at the idea of the bathroom her heart began beating a little strangely. "I know everything about you, you're a poor lonely woman with no education and a hare-lip." The bathroom was suffused with a glimmering twilight, and when Amanda entered, all the noise of the airport faded. Inside, a woman with a harelip was washing the floor, stooped over as she dragged a rag across the tile, and she was singing "Oy oy oy!" to the tune of Amanda's song.

"What's that you're singing?" Amanda whispered.

"Oy oy oy!" hummed the woman, almost viciously, then looked up at Amanda with her cloudy gray eyes. "It's a song, see?" and she went on scrubbing the floor.

Amanda flew to Moscow. Life lost its colors for her: recording and performing, trips and clubs, her boyfriend, her cosmetologist, tanning and shopping and whatever else she had loved—all of it had turned out to be a trick, a lie, because somewhere in eastern Siberia there lived a woman with a harelip and Amanda's handwriting, her signature, her song. Amanda's entire life was ruined, poisoned, revealed to be a hoax, someone's cruel joke.

Then Amanda threw herself out of a window; nobody knew why. At her funeral there was a woman with a harelip no one recognized. She stood there for a while, then went away.

THE LIFE OF SHAGDAROV

Anatoly Sergeyevich Shagdarov was born in the Soviet Socialist Republic of Buryatia, in one of the urban settlements on the shores of Lake Baikal, which had an asphalt plant, two water towers, and a pumping station. His grandfather on his mother's side was a shaman, his father was a Russian alcoholic, and his mother died when Shagdarov was five years old, from tick-borne encephalitis. His father didn't mourn his first wife and soon brought home a Russian stepmother, and when people asked about the mother of little Shagdarov, he said only that she was "dark."

As a teenager, during the war, Shagdarov herded goats and thought about the universe: Why it is the way it is, why it exists at all. After the war he studied at the agri-technical college and worked as the chief animal technician on a collective farm in Irkutsk Oblast. He had a wife there, dark, like his mother, who sang folk songs, and later fell ill and wasted away without leaving him any children. After her death, the thirty-year-old Shagdarov decided to become a philosopher and resolve everything about the universe, and he left the collective farm and his animals, and went off to enter a philosophy department in Moscow.

Animal tech Shagdarov grasped the intricacies of philosophy, completed the postgraduate course, and stayed on at the university to teach Marxism-Leninism. Later, he defended his doctoral dissertation, became head of the department, and married a light-haired Muscovite woman, who bore him a son. The students loved Shagdarov because he was wise and kind, and though he knew more than their other professors, he was genuine and friendly with everyone. He spent three years in Cuba, serving as advisor to the rector of the university, saw Fidel Castro, shook his hand, and came home again—and then perestroika started.

In the '90s, Shagdarov's department was renamed the Department of Contemporary Foreign Philosophy, and the now-elderly Shagdarov began mastering the post-structuralists. With his customary enthusiasm, he now lectured students on Derrida and Deleuze. The younger lecturers now smoked right in the auditorium, putting out their cigarettes on the soles of their shoes. One day, as Shagdarov was telling the first-years about Ludwig Wittgenstein, two pretty female students started making love, and at this point Shagdarov had a heart attack. He was taken to the hospital, and there Shagdarov expired.

Present at his funeral were his wife, son, daughter-in-law, and little grandson, as well as many friends, colleagues, and students; people spoke warmly of him and drank vodka, and a student of his, one of the accidental assassins, sobbed in a corner, while the other one hadn't come.

Shagdarov's grandson grew frightened when he saw Granddad in a coffin, and also began to cry, and he didn't know about any of the things his grandfather hadn't had time to tell him:

about the two dark women who died—his mother and his first wife—or about Marx, Lenin, and Fidel Castro, or Derrida and Deleuze, or the reason philosophy had been necessary to an animal technician from a distant collective farm, in those parts where nobody now remembers Shagdarov, just as they've forgotten him in his hometown on the shores of Lake Baikal. Although the local women there still tell stories of his grandfather, and they say he was a powerful shaman.

EXIST A LITTLE

N didn't have a personality per se, not because of social formations, but because of his own personal qualities. He also didn't have a soul per se, not because God is unjust, but because of his particular spiritual attributes. He also didn't have a mind per se, not because of inadequate education, but because of his own intellectual abilities. He didn't have a body per se, not because he'd been slighted by nature, but because of his own physical characteristics. What a guy N was! It's hard to even imagine. There was one consolation for him, however: it was no one's fault.

So what did N actually have? Per se, nothing. Per se, N didn't really exist. He told himself: "At least I'm responsible for that—not society, not God, not nature, just me, it's all because of me." It's possible that N was wrong, and society, God, and nature had deprived him of everything and demoted him to the status of non-being, but N stubbornly insisted that it was all because of him—and although, please allow me to reiterate, N didn't really exist per se—in that sense, N did exist, a little.

THE TREE

A New Year's Trip

In the days when humans were just beginning to explore the far reaches of the universe, Captain Bill Ray was traveling to collect samples from planet S4 in the Agona Galaxy. It was New Year's Eve back on Earth, and Captain Ray was missing the family he'd left behind. On the way to S4, he kept encountering alien beings in carriages (only Earthlings still used clunky starships to get around, the rest of universe had moved on to lighter transportation), and these aliens asked him: "Are you headed to the New Year's Tree?"

"What New Year's Tree?" Captain Ray replied.

"Really, you've never been to the Tree?" the aliens marveled. "You Earthlings, from a planet so far out on the outskirts, have never once been to New Year's, the biggest party in the cosmos?"

"But the new year comes at a different time for everyone," Captain Ray protested.

"At New Year's, every world has a path to the tree," the aliens told him. "So when it's New Year's Eve in our world, we fly to the Tree—and you should, too, since a being who's never visited the Tree isn't clued in to—well—the most important thing, if you know what we mean. It's like taking LSD."

"But where am I supposed to fly?" Captain Ray asked.

"What do you mean, where? To the center of the cosmos," said the aliens.

"But where is that located?" Captain Ray didn't understand.

"What difference does that make," the aliens said. "Just keep going, it'll turn up."

Captain Ray flew on, and after a few parsecs he saw an enormous Tree rising up through space. Its branches grew in tiers and were lavishly decorated, and around the Tree there was a public celebration. Creatures from all kinds of different worlds—humanoids, reptilians, metal golems, sentient oysters—were celebrating the New Year, pouring champagne, shooting off fireworks. Captain Ray spent an eternity circling the Tree in his starship and studying the decorations. There was a sea star spreading its five arms, a seashell, and an octopus; an enormous raspberry and a little bell; every species of bird that had ever existed, fashioned from papier-mâché; a golden pretzel; a grandfather clock with a cuckoo; nuts and pinecones; a golden heart, as well as every other kind of human organ made from precious stones; a steam train and an airplane; a bus and a metro car; his grandfather's opera glasses and a glass lantern; an emerald cucumber and a mahogany guitar; a nutcracker Captain Ray had had as a child, and along with it all the characters from the fairy tales he'd read back then; a teapot and a shoe; a polar bear made of sugar and a piece of candy wrapped with a bow; artificial snow; various geometric shapes: a cube, a cone, and strangely bent, complex figures, like ones in paintings by avant-garde artists; and, of course, there were balls: the golden sphere from the Vatican, the planets, eyeballs. Higher than all of these, above the forms of things, hung several tiers of angels: the Angels, Archangels, and Principalities, the Powers, Virtues, and Dominions, and Ophanim, Cherubim, and Seraphim. Crucified Christ hung there, and smiling Buddha, and the prophet Muhammad. And when Captain Ray rose higher than everything that existed, he saw God wedged onto the top of the tree in the form of an old, bearded man in a majestically shining crown—awesome, but a toy.

All around, the creatures of the cosmos frolicked like children. A tipsy sentient oyster in the neighboring carriage was trying to hit on a snake woman. Rock music was coming from other carriages and various beings were dancing to it, and Captain Ray felt simultaneously happy and sad. He was happy because it seemed like some heavy burden had been lifted from him, and he felt light and free and united in shared abandonment with all of his accidental companions from the infinite reaches of the universe. And he was sad because he had remembered his family and his home, and he felt lonelier by this Tree than he had ever felt before, as though he were in a giant nursery, and his parents had left him. And Captain Ray began to cry. Then a barking bubble from planet Gamma 3895 flew up to him and yipped: "It's amazing, right? Everyone gets like this the first time they see it. I've been coming every year for two hundred and ninety years. It fucks you up pretty good, I'd say."

TO THE CORE

Yegor, who until then had been making a brilliant scientific career, began undergoing electroshock therapy treatments that rendered him unable to remember anything. When he finally began remembering things again, he wondered whether he'd still have anything to think about, or whether everything had become clear to him forever. Back home at his parents' place, he realized that he now understood all things down to their core, but he couldn't do science anymore.

"What am I going to do now?" he asked his mother.

"You'll get better and go back to work at your university," she said, timidly.

"No, Mother," said Yegor, "I can see things down to their core now, which means I can't do science. In order to do science, you have to see things through a fog of ignorance and discovery."

"Well, if that's the case, there are lots of simple, not particularly taxing jobs," his mother said. "You could be a coatroom attendant or a janitor at your same university. After all, all jobs are worthy of respect, and a coatroom attendant is just as good as a scientist. All jobs have to be done with care."

"Mother," said Yegor, "you're reasoning like an intellectual, because behind your love of the common man there's condescension, and deep down you don't believe anyone except so-called intellectuals is capable of thought."

"That's your depression talking," said Yegor's mother, "but you'll get better soon."

"I'm fine now," Yegor protested. "Do you know why I agreed to undergo electroshock therapy? I wanted the electric charge to restore the molecules in my mind to their proper places, the places they occupied in our pure, primordial state, so they could revive and produce their harmonic resonance, which I can hear in my mind as a beautiful song."

"And what about the voices in your head, do you still hear them?" his mother asked with concern.

Yegor sighed. He was used to people falling into one of two groups: the nominalists and the realists. He knew that one group considered love to be blindness and that the other considered it to be illumination. One group thought art gave rise to illusions, while the other thought art put us in direct contact with reality. Even as he was losing his mind, Yegor believed that his hallucinations weren't the random fluctuations of an ailing consciousness, but evidence of the way human reasoning and the world really worked.

Yegor put on a pair of sunglasses and went outside. All around him lay creation without a creator. At the store where he bought a pack of cigarettes, the clerk asked him why he was wearing sunglasses in winter, and he replied: "I don't want to see you down to your very core—taking a look and burning you to ashes through the very act of looking."

Yegor walked down the street smoking and looking at the buildings in the snow, the bums, the bent old women—and seeing, at the same time, a prelinguistic ocean of fragments, seaweed, muck, and salt, in which meanings were engendered and stars were born. Meanings were created and passed away; some lasted for ages, hundreds of years, others for a fraction of a second. The bodies of stars put forth growths like the buds of plants, the buds sprang open, and new stars grew on the bodies of the old, then slowly detached from them. Yegor saw all of this and knew that he could remain forever in this ocean, spending eons among the silt-covered stars and sunken ships . . . and he did not return to science and went instead among the people, working as a train manager on the Moscow-Vladivostok line. He was happy there, but he always wore his sunglasses, in order not to see to the core of those who were not ready for such a thing.

SONGS OF
THE BLIND BEGGARS

A blind beggar once told Mikhail Ilyich about the land of the Mother Dove. It happened like this: on one of the first icy days of the year, Mikhail Ilyich saw an old, blind man trying to cross the street. He had a white cane he was using to tap through space, and he was dressed like someone on the lowest rungs of society. He was coming from the direction of the metro, where he spent his days singing in the underground crossing. Mikhail Ilyich helped him cross, and the blind man said to him, "You've helped me, but am I really blind?"

"Of course you're blind," said Mikhail Ilyich. "You can't see the world around you, the houses, the garbage dump, the shopping center by the metro stop, or this road, covered in ice."

"That's true, I can't see those things," the blind man agreed, "but I can see the land of the Mother Dove. I see beautiful estates, forests, fields, hills, and dovecotes."

The blind old man went on his way, and Mikhail Ilyich began to lament that he himself couldn't see the land of the Mother Dove. He lamented this all through December and January, and in February he woke up early one morning and looked out the window. Beyond the window were bare branches, the courtyard, sixteen-story apartment blocks. He left his apartment to go to work and suddenly noticed, by an iced-over puddle near the local kindergarten, a gathering flock of pigeons. They were all different colors—blue-gray, snow-white, nearly lilac—and as soon as they appeared, everything took on a softer, more benevolent cast, in the sky and on the earth, as though his own long-dead mother were smiling at him. Beautiful forests and dovecotes began to glimmer through the haze of the winter day, as though one roll of film had been superimposed over another. In this way, Mikhail Ilyich gained true sight. There were many more times throughout his life when the land of the Mother Dove appeared to him, and he came to understand the songs of the blind beggars.

THE INSECT PRIEST

There once was a village where the priest was really an insect, but the congregation had no idea. This village was tucked away in a hollow in the mountains, several hours' walk, through swampland, from the nearest highway. The village was home to eight villagers and six monks who lived in a crumbling Old Believers' monastery. The villagers all attended services at the monastery and were God-fearing folk. There was no cell service in those parts, except in one single spot, on the mountainside near the monastery, from which calls could be made. The village priest taught his flock that they would be saved as long as they kept the three commandments: 1) Thou shalt not use a SIM card; 2) Thou shalt not use an electric kettle; 3) Thou shalt not use bug spray.

One day, two demons, Abaddon and his girlfriend Naamah, having heard that these villagers were saved and their priest was deeply devout, assumed the guises of a young man and woman and decided to journey to this village to corrupt the faithful. Every day, they went to the monastery and made calls on their cell phones right in front of the monks; they heated water in an electric kettle, and once, as the priest was leading the evening service, Naamah ran up to him and sprayed him with bug spray. The priest transformed into a gigantic insect, and the demons fled the monastery and ran cackling through the swamp in the direction of the highway, where they flagged down a passing car, got in, and drove away.

Then the villagers fell into temptation and began to doubt their priest. They started using cell phones and electric kettles and referring to the priest strictly as Bug Daddy, and a few times somebody even tried to break into the monastery to spray insecticide. Nobody was saved in that village any longer. Abaddon and Naamah moved to Moscow, where they started hanging out at hipster spots, drinking craft beer, and listening to trendy music. And in the meantime, even now, legions of demons on the airwaves, assisted by a supercomputer at the NATO headquarters in Brussels, go on driving people to sin; legions of demons enter the drinking water through the coils of electric kettles and possess people; legions of demons assailing the far-flung villages of Holy Rus are kept at bay only by the beetle-priests, spider-priests, praying-mantis-priests—confessors of the faith, pilgrims, and praying saints.

DONT SAY IM A GODES

The Sex Pest was looking for his love. He approached women in the street, introduced himself, got their numbers, then sent lewd texts suggesting they meet up and sleep together. He was a rehab doctor who made house calls to wealthy clients recovering from injuries and strokes, and on the way to these appointments he would inevitably pester several women.

One day, the Sex Pest hit on a tall, beautiful woman—the Mean Girl. She initially refused to give him her number, but then gave in, because, first of all, she was in a hurry and that was the only way to get rid of the Sex Pest, and second, she liked telling annoying men to fuck off over text. But she grew tired of the Sex Pest pretty quickly. Morning, noon, and night the Sex Pest texted her: *I want to have sex with you / How much would you charge to screw you / You need a good fuck / Let's smash*, and so on. The Mean Girl kept telling him off, but then realized it was better to ignore him and stopped responding, and after some time the Sex Pest left her alone.

The Sex Pest forgot about the Mean Girl and didn't think of her until about six months later, when he saw her number in his phone and couldn't remember who she was. So he started texting her again: *Who are you? / Why do I have your number? / Let's meet! / Send me a photo*—and gave her his email address. The Mean Girl emailed him a picture of the Big Girl, writing: *heres my pic. dont say im a godes i aldredy know. we can link up.* The Mean Girl had run into the Big Girl a couple of times when they were both in school; the Big Girl was a classmate of one of the Mean Girl's friends. And the Mean Girl found recent pictures of her online. The Big Girl was astonishingly, amazingly large. The Mean Girl sent the Sex Pest the Big Girl's photo from a fake account, then deleted the account, and after that the Sex Pest didn't text her anymore.

A few years later, the Mean Girl saw the Big Girl on an escalator, but she wasn't absolutely sure it was her, particularly because the Big Girl was supposed to be living in Omsk, where both the women were from, and where the Big Girl had a job as a salesclerk. "Maybe she moved? But who actually cares," the Mean Girl wondered idly, and went on with her day. She had no inkling that it was all thanks to her that the Big Girl now led a happy life in Moscow.

Three years prior, when the Sex Pest opened the file containing the Big Girl's picture . . . I can't even describe what happened next. Basically, the Sex Pest immediately realized that the Big Girl was the woman he had been searching for his entire life. He was certain that the photo wasn't of the woman whose number was in his phone, because if he'd come across the woman in the photo he never would have forgotten her. He started searching for the picture online, found the Big Girl on social media, began writing to her, went to Omsk, convinced her to move in with him in Moscow, and married her. They were both very happy, and when their friends, and later their children, asked Mommy and Daddy how they'd met, the Sex Pest would say, "One day I went online, and some anonymous person had sent me a picture of your mother! I fell in love with her on the spot, looked for her and found her, and then you were born." The Big Girl had no idea who could have sent the Sex Pest her picture. She didn't even know the Mean Girl existed. At the end of the day, both the Sex Pest and the Big Girl attributed their meeting to God and Providence. In this way, the paths of the Mean Girl, the Big Girl, and the Sex Pest crossed, and love abounded on the earth.

IVAN KUZMICH IN THE UNIVERSE OF POINTS

Ivan Kuzmich—sixth-rank mechanical assembly fitter at the Precision Machinery Plant, and a philosopher and mystic in his spare time—read on the internet one night that our universe is a hologram, and that none of us really exist.

"If you say so," Ivan Kuzmich thought to himself. "But like it or not, here I am." Broadly speaking, however, he understood the theory. It was based on the fairly recent proposition that time and space in the universe are not continuous. They consist of discrete parts—points, similar to pixels. That's why, as Ivan Kuzmich understood it, an image of the universe can't be expanded infinitely, allowing us to look deeper and deeper into the essence of things. All of which means, Ivan Kuzmich grasped, that at a certain scale the universe is something like a very low-resolution digital image.

From beneath his pillow, Ivan Kuzmich took out a magazine with a picture of a naked woman on the cover.

"Let's say this is the universe," he said, addressing the invisible interlocutor he had imagined.

"What a cow," the invisible interlocutor commented, regarding the naked woman.

"Scram, quit bothering me, son of a bitch!" Ivan Kuzmich banished his apparently unenlightened interlocutor, then imagined him back again.

"As I was saying," he continued, gazing at the photograph, "this is the universe. It looks like a continuous, uninterrupted image, but at a certain level of magnification it dissolves into the points that compose the unified whole. And it's the same way with our world," the amateur philosopher continued happily, "which is composed of microscopic points that form a single beautiful image!"

Ivan Kuzmich smacked his lips, went to the window, and stood there admiring the single beautiful image of a universe composed of microscopic points. The image consisted of houses, snowbanks, snow-covered cars, a kindergarten nearly invisible in the darkness of the courtyard, and the greenish moon, hazy in its eternal limbo, its light spilling forth onto a slanted, snow-laden apple tree near the ground-floor window. Ivan Kuzmich felt like howling at the moon like a wolf, howling because of how lonely he felt faced with this beautiful universe he had nearly figured out. One thing still puzzled him: What was behind the hologram? How did it come to be?

The online article that Ivan Kuzmich had read said that science was not equipped to answer such questions. Maybe it would be able to answer them someday, but most likely it wouldn't. Human understanding is inadequate. The President of the Royal Society in London, cosmologist and astrophysicist Martin Rees, a thoroughgoing pessimist, said as much: "Any universe complicated enough to have allowed our emergence is for just that reason too complicated for our minds to understand."

"What do you mean, too complicated?" rebelled the more-than-adequate mind of Ivan Kuzmich. "What about my mind? What about me? Just tell me, I'll get the gist right away." In this mood, Ivan Kuzmich went to bed, having firmly decided to grasp in his sleep whatever remained to be grasped about the universe, and to wake in the full knowledge of it—perhaps for the enlightenment of humanity, or maybe just to store the knowledge in the solitude of his own soul.

In his dreams, Ivan Kuzmich's mind found itself in a space before time, where all things began. By his side was the great sixteenth-century Kabbalist Isaac Luria, whose soul had harkened to the call of Ivan Kuzmich's soul and now undertook to show him the greatest secrets of the universe. And Ivan Kuzmich saw how, emanating from the Ein Sof, Divine Light flowed into the boundless space of the tzimtzum—which God had created by contracting into Himself, and where the foundation of the world was laid—not in separate streams, but in a unified, precise and pointed, laser-like beam. And a man was formed from this light, and Isaac Luria told Ivan Kuzmich that this was Adam Kadmon. Light streamed from Adam Kadmon's eyes, lips, ears, and nose. These streams united into a single whole, but the light that emanated from Adam Kadmon's eyes remained diffuse, and each sefirah formed an individual point.

"Look, brother, this is what you were wondering about," said Luria. "This is the world of light points, Olam HaNekudim."

Waking at dawn, Ivan Kuzmich first forgot everything and then remembered it all. He went to the window again and looked at the dawn breaking over Moscow. He knew that the dawn consisted of points, just like all the houses and the cars, and the snow on the branches of the apple tree beneath his window, and the sparrows, too. Looking into the sky, as though trying to see through it to the very dawn itself, to the distant planets and stars, Ivan Kuzmich understood that within him had formed the point at which humanity had arrived. He saw the invisible like a visionary, reasoned like a philosopher, and burned to test and analyze everything like a scientist, all of which meant that he, a lonely mechanical assembly fitter of the sixth rank, had achieved the first-rank self-awareness of mankind.

He knew that he wouldn't be able to prove any of this to anyone, but he hoped that in the near future scientists would invent a device that would disprove everything humanity knew about the universe before the start of Ivan Kuzmich's research. This device would prove that the universe as we knew it did not exist, that the universe is actually Divine light, Ein Sof, forming Adam Kadmon and his eyes, which in turn create the world of points, giving rise to the universal hologram. The hologram contains all elementary particles and every possible form of matter and energy: snowflakes and quarks, blue whales and gamma rays. The device would also prove that humans as a species don't exist, and rather that there is only continuous nirvana.

Until such a device was invented, Ivan Kuzmich decided to keep his knowledge to himself. Once, out drinking, he wanted to share it with his friend, the plumber Fyodor Petrovich, and he opened his mouth to speak, but said only, "Oh, man," and waved his hand.

THE TRICYCLE AND THE RUBBER DILDO

A man and a woman ran into each other by the entrance of their building. The man was tall, wearing sweatpants and a red T-shirt. He was carrying a tricycle, and, seeing it, the woman thought, "He's a good father, you can tell. Not like my ex, who left me alone with a kid and won't pay child support. This guy's carrying a bike, he probably takes his son to school, plays soccer with him." Imagining the ideal happiness of this man's family life, the woman felt envious and annoyed.

Over her shoulder, the woman was carrying a fairly large black purse, about which the man thought: "There's a woman's burden. What the hell are they all carrying around in these giant purses, anyway? None other than the chains of space and time, all the world's sorrow, some enormous book that's only full of nonsense."

Both of them searched for their keys for a long time, glancing at each other suspiciously. Finally, one of them found the fob, held it to the reader, and they entered the building. The man with the tricycle pushed the button for the elevator, while the woman walked to her apartment on the first floor. The man with the tricycle rode the elevator to the top floor, to his bachelor's apartment. He didn't have a son; he had stolen the tricycle from the neighboring courtyard—he had a habit of stealing various things and bringing them home.

The woman went inside, fed her son, and retired to her room. From her large black bag, she withdrew a large black box, which contained a large black rubber dildo, and used it as intended, forgetting her poverty and her loneliness. She had a son, and he needed a father and a tricycle, and the man on the top floor had a tricycle and a penis and no one to share them with. The man put the tricycle into a small, cluttered room that was more like a storage closet; the woman put the rubber dildo back into its box.

THE CEMETERY
OF OUR DREAMS

Two sullen, hard-faced women, mother and daughter, one past fifty, the other around thirty, rode their bikes up to the funeral bureau in the village of Sosnovo. This bureau is located on the grounds of the local hospital, just left of the entrance; surrounding the hospital is a pine forest. The women dismounted and leaned their bicycles against the wall of the building. Both were dressed shoddily, village-style, indifferent to their appearance, in granny pants and old, plain sweaters. The daughter wore a kerchief on her head, as though she were going to church. Their drawn faces were frozen in an expression of mute tension.

The women knocked on the door, cracked it open, and looked in. Inside sat a plump, made-up lady, talking to some man. "You have to wait," she said to the women. Obediently, they shut the door and stood very straight next to it, waiting. They had been standing silently in this way for about seven minutes when the door finally opened, the man walked out, and they were admitted to the premises.

"Good afternoon," said the mother. "We'd like to find out whether it's possible to bury a body at the Sosnovo cemetery." For anyone not in the know, the Sosnovo cemetery is located near the hospital, in the pine forest. It's quaint and picturesque, with tall pines growing between the graves.

"You've had someone die that you want to bury? A local, from Sosnovo?" asked the lady from the bureau.

"We just want to find out," said the women. "For ourselves."

"Are you sick?" asked the surprised bureau lady.

"No, we're relatively healthy," said the daughter. "We just want to know."

"Are you local?" the lady asked.

"Our dacha is in the next village over, but our permanent registration is in Petersburg," the women told her.

"Then it's not allowed," said the lady. "We have a municipal cemetery here. We only bury people who are registered as living in Sosnovo."

"We'd really like it," said the daughter, "we're so fond of this cemetery. The pines are there, and it seems like such a nice place to rest. And for the people who would visit, it would be so pleasant to sit by the graves beneath the trees, drinking wine, reminiscing. Is it really not allowed?"

"No, it's not," said the lady sternly, "we bury ONLY locals."

"We can pay," said the mother. "Maybe it's allowed for money?"

"No, it's not allowed," the lady yelled, "we bury ONLY locals! Only locals! There's no room at the cemetery, so there are no paid plots. It's a municipal cemetery, we bury people for free, but only from Sosnovo."

"But we were told," the mother continued monotonously,

"that for money you could go anywhere, even the Alexander Nevsky Lavra."

"No," shouted the bureau lady, "it's not allowed, it's a municipal cemetery, there's no room!" Then, looking at the mother and daughter's suffering expressions, she added, a touch more gently, "Right now it's not allowed. But who knows what'll happen later? Say more land gets allotted to cemetery, then maybe we *will* be allowed to bury city folks for money. These days the laws change every other month! Who can say what's going to happen? Maybe it will be allowed, later. You go live for now," the lady said even more gently, with feeling, "and maybe you'll live until the time when we can bury you."

The conversation was over. The women said goodbye and walked out with the same expressions of tension and a kind of deep-rooted suffering on their faces, got on their bicycles, and rode away.

SOME BULLSHIT

The nonsense that goes on sometimes, you don't even know what to call it. It's some bullshit, that's all you can say. Total bullshit. It starts slowly, then picks up speed. For instance, one day Pavel started noticing odd little incidents. Things not adding up. His wedding ring had always been yellow gold, but one day he looked at it and it was made of white gold. Bullshit. And his wife says, "Did you hit your head? We've always had white-gold rings." Or, suddenly, his computer mouse: it used to be wireless and now it's this dumb one with a cord. And his son says, "You've always had that kind of mouse."

And the changes keep coming. Pavel and his wife and son are coming home from their dacha, it's a nice autumn evening, they're walking through the courtyards, Pavel looks at the block where he grew up, its trees, streetlamps, old apartment houses, and suddenly he sees his wife and son turning left, going to the entrance of one of those apartment houses, the second entrance. Pavel says, "Where are you going?" And they say, "What do you mean where? We're going home." But they'd always lived in a different building, farther on, by the intersection, a high-rise. Pavel tells them, "We don't live here," but the two of them go, "We've always lived here. You're really losing it, Dad."

Bullshit. Then Pavel's on a work trip from St. Petersburg to Moscow, taking the high-speed train, passing all the usual stations: Okulovka, Bologoye, everything as it should be, but there's no Tver stop. Surprised, Pavel asks the attendant why the train isn't stopping in Tver, and she goes, "What is Tver? There's no such city and there never was." Pavel couldn't believe it, he asked all his friends, looked it up online, studied a map of Russia—and there never was a Tver. And this went on continuously, as though the whole world were slowly changing, bit by bit, or God was rewriting creation as He went, and only Pavel could tell.

There's no point describing in detail all of these unexpected discrepancies as they snowballed. Suffice it to say that finally Pavel discovered that she was a happy Black woman living in the Republic of the Congo in the twenty-third century, and everyone around insisted that this had always been the case.

SWEAR ON A BEAR

Little Timoshka's grandmother always told him: "Never swear on a bear." Everyone in his family knew not to do it; his mother knew, and his aunts, and they also reminded him, at every opportunity: "Just don't swear on a bear." Anything else was allowed, in principle. It was all right to lie or to tell the truth, just as you liked, so long as you didn't swear on a bear.

As Grandma said, speech is a dangerous and dirty thing, and even when you tell the truth with a clear conscience, someone else will certainly suffer because of it. Swearing is the most ancient way to assert that something is true, and it's doubly dangerous, because it also implicates the person you're calling to witness. And you don't want to fool around with a bear. Go ahead and swear on your honor, your name, your life, on God—so Grandma said—and that's all fine, that's nothing. But don't ever swear on a bear. A bear is real, a bear is absolute, you can never make a bear the stakes in a symbolic struggle, you'll never drag a bear into a language game. Anything spoken is a human matter, the arena of struggle and recognition. You can say anything you want, lie as easy as you breathe, but remember, dear grandson, the bear has nothing to do with it, therefore you should never swear on a bear.

Timoshka grew up an inveterate liar and teller of tales. "Mama, can I tell a girl I love her so she'll let me copy?" Timoshka asked his mother before an algebra test.

"Sure, darling, just don't swear on a bear," his mother said. Everything else went the same way. Running his mouth got Timoshka into a philosophy department and then to his dissertation defense. His dissertation was on contemporary French philosophy, and at the defense an extraordinary incident occurred that was discussed in academic circles for a long time afterward. The members of Timoshka's committee gathered for the defense, including one elderly Marxist-Leninist woman who by this time was quite senile. Timoshka started defending his work, and the Marxist-Leninist started trying to catch him out: "Do I understand correctly that you mean *this* here, while Lenin wrote just the opposite?" And so on. Timoshka rebutted and rebutted, until he grew tired, started sweating buckets, and the Marxist-Leninist lady finally got him. She said, "So you think that perception is *not* reflection?" Timoshka nearly fainted at this nonsense and didn't know how he should respond. He thought any idiot knew that perception was *not* reflection, that was plain as day, but now she was demanding that he say it, and with an edge, too. He replied, with an excess of feeling, "It's really not, I swear on a bear." Then an enormous bear burst into the auditorium, grabbed the doctoral candidate and dragged him from his defense into the woods, into another world. There Timoshka made his home in a swamp and became a cannibal prince.

MAN AND BRICK

There lived a man who always took the same way to work and back. In one particular spot above his route hung a brick. The brick had been suspended above the road, right in the very sky, by the Lord himself. This man walked back and forth beneath the brick, never giving it a second thought, until one morning his wife yelled at him. After their argument, the man walked down the road out of sorts, glanced at the brick, and felt a vague sense of unease.

"God," he said, addressing the sky, "I see you've hung a brick above the road. Generally speaking, I don't mind, it's none of my business and all, but please allow me to inquire—what are the chances this brick will up and fall on my head?"

"Man," said God, "don't worry about it, live your life, the chance of that brick falling on your head is about one in thirty million."

From that day on the man had no peace. He stopped going to work and couldn't even get near the brick. He kept thinking:

"But what if it falls?" The Devil caught wind of this and decided to help the man out.

"God," said the Devil, "that man is suffering, it hurts to even look at him. Get rid of that damn brick."

"I can't," said God. "I willed that it would hang in that spot back before time began. Nothing to be done about it now. And that man is suffering because he's an idiot. I already told him that the chance of the brick falling on his head is one out of thirty million. He has absolutely nothing to worry about."

"You don't know people very well," said the Devil. "But fine, now I think I know how to help him. Make it so that the chances of the brick falling are fifty percent—it will either fall or it won't." God shrugged and did as the Devil asked.

Then the Devil went to the man and said, "Have you heard? The brick above the road now has a fifty percent chance of falling on your head—it will either fall or it won't."

The man immediately calmed down and stopped worrying. "Whatever, maybe it won't fall," he said to the Devil, and walked serenely beneath the brick on his way to work. The brick really didn't fall. Then the man walked home from work, once again taking the road that passed beneath the brick.

"Hey, Man!" God called to him. "You shouldn't walk there, there's a fifty-percent chance that brick falls on your head!"

"Maybe not though," said the man, and passed serenely beneath the brick. The next day he headed down the road beneath the brick for the third time.

"Man! Don't walk there!" God shouted to him. "There's a high probability the brick will fall on your head, and this is the third time you've walked under it."

"Maybe it won't," said the man, and kept walking. The brick fell and broke open his head. The Devil took his soul. Then God picked up the brick and hung it back up in its prior place, where it remains to this day, with a one-in-thirty-million chance of falling.

A PORTRAIT OF
THE ARTIST AT THIRTY

There once lived a woman named X. At thirty she still didn't know how to earn a living, network, establish a suitable place for herself in life, change her circumstances, be the first to end a relationship, or choose a wine or any other luxury consumer good. She had no idea how or where to pay her rent or utilities, couldn't understand tax deductions, and felt deeply ignorant when people around her discussed politics, economics, or philosophy (even though she'd studied philosophy for eight years, graduated with honors, and was told her dissertation was the best in the history of the department). X couldn't see the point of creative nonfiction and could hardly read books, because they were all "words, words, words" (yet she herself wrote poetry and prose). For five years straight, laboriously and through sheer force of will, she read only Andrey Platonov, because everything else only skimmed the surface of her consciousness and never penetrated her soul. While X's friends dreamed of rich, edgy boyfriends, her ideal man had about him something of the village schoolteacher and something of a young Protestant pastor: strict, selfless, honorable, impassioned, and filled with an abiding faith in his preemptively lost cause. What *did* she know how to do? Write so-called classics, control dreams, fuck, keep friendships going, drink without getting drunk, hike up mountains without complaining, work long, hard hours for very little money, teach something nobody needed to people who didn't give a shit, not work at all and be happy, withstand hellish torments for some time without committing suicide. When X was in school she could jump higher than everyone else in her special medical needs group in gym class. And that is probably all.

ON THAT DAY HE LEARNED

On that day he learned the answer to everything he'd been wondering his entire life. Now he knew why the sky was blue and the grass was green, and why deep, powdery snow keeps winter grains from freezing. In the sky above the Olgino train platform, flocks of birds were flying south, one after another. He was watching them, his head tilted back, when he saw that the flying formations were arranging themselves into letters, then words. At length, the birds overhead clearly spelled out the word MORON, then flew onward.

II

THE WAY TO
THE GALLOWS
RUNS THROUGH
MERRY MEADOWS

THE MAN WITH THE MAGNIFYING GLASS

Ask the rain to fill your buckets with water and you won't need a well. The water in the well is gone anyway, the underground riverbed is dry, and the water is much deeper now than this emptied subterranean lake. Dig in the earth, and you'll find the water deeper down.

Go and feed the gadflies by the Istrut River. Descend into the thicket of nettles and burdock, but be careful: Not long ago, in a furrow in the field, a snake lay crushed by a tractor. There are snakes here, but you're wandering blindly into grass that's half as tall as you are, carrying soap and shampoo, on your way to bathe in the river. It's shallow there, all pebbles and sand, and you, naked to the waist, have a mosquito net, but the mosquitos bite you anyway.

Go and feed the midges on the Ay River. There's a family of drunks on the riverbank; they came out here in an ATV to go fishing. Their shouts echo and spread. The kid has gone off somewhere, and the mother says, "Where is he, that little bastard? We're going the fuck home!" The drunk father roars, "Slavka, you motherfucker, come here!" Later, there's the sound of a child crying, people cursing, a kid screaming, "Papa, don't, I already got it!"

In this strange mixture of paradise and nightmare you're still partly in the garden where everything blooms and expands, a sprawling jungle of nettles, a garden that perhaps only the old botanist can find—the man with the magnifying glass, that peculiar being who returns us to our childhood. You'll grow up to be like your parents, or if you're not quite like them, maybe a little bottle of antidepressants will take up residence in your bathroom cabinet, and you'll keep searching for a way back into the garden, the little garden where everything grows so big, my God, it's enormous!

Devote your dreams to the butterfly that flutters from the shell you find on the beach: the way it slowly emerges, its wings folded, opening them as it rests on your palm . . . The butterfly flits above black waves capped with white foam. Dream of the stone-tailed fairy when you find a snail after the rain. Who knows—maybe from this shell, too, a horned butterfly will emerge? *Melusina*— you remember the name.

Maybe you want to live among the cats, among the deep rumbling coming from the pile of old newspapers beneath the bed, behind the stove, in the corner. You want to savor true poverty, the kind that's more precious than gold. I asked: "What lives in the Ay River? What kinds of fish?" You told me: "Chub and grayling." Last year we ate chub, and we argued for a long time about who would clean it. If you remove everything—cut off the head, the fins, strip the scales, toss the bones—there's so little left that the effort no longer seems worth it.

The man with the magnifying glass, the handler of heaven, taught me one thing: to look closely at the roots of nettle, hogweed, burdock, dandelions, the plantain by the road. How the little spiderwebs wreathing the turnips glow! Is this chirring crimson-pink creature really a cricket? Aren't crickets green? And the wind, you can see it—it's that flickering motion in the corner of your eye. Notice the little rings and flares that hover in the air, a faint white luminescence around the trees. If you look closely, in the sky at around the height of your forehead you'll notice a pulsing, wide-open funnel-flower with fan-blade petals. And, afterward, you'll be more sensitive to smells and better able to see.

The rustle of a bird fluttering up from the tall grass, the bushes by the fence. The ancient little banya is barely visible in the undergrowth. "Where does fog come from?" we ask one another. Sometimes it arrives in the evening, spreads along the fields, encircles us like a blockade. It comes down from the mountains and floats up out of the overgrown, empty pond. Sometimes it comes in the early morning, again from the fields, the mountains, and before dawn it's been mown by the enchanted scythes that belong to the silent reapers of fog. The cut sheaves float on as inspiration.

Do you remember the trolley that took us through the city of Zlatoust, in the mountains? We could see it all through the windows—the crests of the Taganay range and the enormous city pond. The mountains' evergreen slopes alternated with the urban sprawl, and we could see that Zlatoust was an agglomeration of many scattered parts, between which the wilderness seemed to leave no room for people. The city baffled the imagination—it must be what the urban life of the future will be like.

The rails turned at the foot of the mountains, by an old yellow-white house where I could have lived happily for all eternity. The real secret, the riddle, alluringly left unsaid: What lies beyond the house? Where do the tracks go? Maybe bliss itself lies along that path, the coziest and most secluded corners of the city. Where the domain of the soul begins. A green realm, sunlit, with little old houses along the road and astonishingly bright grass sprouting up between the trolley tracks.

Incidentally, there's such a thing as horizontal rain. Everyone knows about rain that comes down slant, but it can also rain across. It's something like a tree that grows downward, or the time when buds bloomed on an elm and put forth not needles but leaves. Or like the butterfly that came from the shell you found, remember? I've always dreamed of being caught in horizontal rain, and today it happened: only the left half of me got wet. And in the spring, after the blueberries ripen, spruce trees bloom at the dacha. Horizontal rain, blooming spruces, elm leaves, butterflies in shells—all miracles performed by the man with the magnifying glass. He must be an educated man, a botanist, a geometer, a logician, a poet . . .

But these are also miracles fit for the child who likes to listen to the grass growing, the mice running in the cellar, the spider hiding beneath the bed. The man with the magnifying glass is the keeper of the gates to a world where grass has more insight than man, ushering on the departed as they move along the flat earth toward a starry slope. In the season's first frost a rabbit in a furrow looks beyond the horizon. And laughing voices from beneath the roots of an old spruce are calling out to you, mortal.

CAN YOU SEE
MY DRAGONS?

Sometimes she asked him, "Can you see my dragons?" The dragons were everywhere: in teardrops and snowdrops, and in drops of rain, in the fire of the hearth and the clumps of earth on his boots. The two of them, he and she, were a Jester and his Joke. The Jester sprouted jokes like the hairs of a beard; one day he sprouted her, and having done so, he fell in love. Above all else, she loved sleeping until the children of the winter rain, who live in puddles, became ice. At night something is always becoming something else, one thing turns into another, here becomes there. The Jester slept next to her, all wrapped up in his long red beard, which was indeed made of jokes. As the Joke went on living with the Jester, she too began to grow a beard; there's a good reason that, in Russian, an old joke is said to be bearded; all jokes begin to grow beards as they grow old. In this way they lived long and happily together, until they became tree stumps, the Jester and his little bearded Joke, in the land of giggles and gigglers, holy fools and happy madmen.

DIPTYCH

I. NOT QUITE

N was born to his mother, a human female, and his father, a human male. He had a body and a mind, like any other person, but he wasn't quite a person, since in order to be a person, you need a little something else. He lived in a place that was composed of a number of buildings, but was not quite a city. Inside his residence (not quite a house) stood a wooden contraption with four legs and a back (not quite a chair), and a large, comfortable, not-quite bed, with a blanket and pillows—since obviously a blanket, four legs, and some pillows don't yet make a bed a bed. He also had a fluffy, whiskery, tabby not-quite-cat—since four paws, whiskers, and a tail clearly are not quite enough to be a cat. Both within N himself, and within everything that surrounded him, something else needed to appear, some symbolic addition. Then things would become themselves, and N would become a person. But that's just what was missing.

II. TOO MUCH

Y, also born to a human woman and a human man, was too much of a person. Driven hopelessly insane by the excess of humanity in him, he lived in a place that had previously been a beautiful city but had lately become an uber-city and lay in ruins. His residence, which had been a perfect house, was wrecked and sat abandoned. For furniture he had a broken too-chair and a rickety too-bed. His too-cat was no longer with him: its death was the culminating achievement of being a cat. In both the madman Y, and in everything that surrounded him, there was a kind of excess, a surplus, which destroyed them—because things are completed when they are ruined.

THE LIVES OF MONSTERS

There once was a guy who was seeing two girls at once, Scylla and Charybdis. They pretended not to know about each other, but really they knew, though they'd never met in person. At night they looked through each other's pictures on social media. In these photos, Charybdis saw very clearly that Scylla had the head of a dog, and that her legs were the tails of fishes, covered in scales. And Scylla saw very clearly that Charybdis was not a woman but a whirlpool. In the watery vortex that was Charybdis, Scylla discerned the desire to get married at any price. And Scylla's fish tails clearly indicated to Charybdis that her rival led a life of debauchery. But this guy didn't see anything like that; from his point of view Scylla and Charybdis were just girls like any other girls, one had really nice breasts, the other a great ass, but he liked Charybdis better because she always paid for herself at the café, and so eventually he married her.

[TH]OUGHTS

Things made out of the mind differ from things made out of matter by virtue of their history. The history of things made out of matter is the story of master and material, the machine and the shop counter. The history of things made out of the mind is the story of the imagination. The two stories proceed in parallel, although sometimes they overlap. For clarity, let's call things made of matter [th]*ings*, and things made of mind [th]*oughts*. In each *ing* there is always at least a little *ought*. The story of matter always contains the story of the imagination. Most people have never seen a pure *ought*, but I have. I love the history of *ings*, but it's possible that one day we will live in a world made entirely of *oughts*. Sometimes I can't tell right away if it's an *ing* or an *ought* in front of me, because at first glance they look the same. Then I start researching the history of this object, and in this way, it becomes clear whether it's an *ing* or an *ought*. But here, too, it's possible to make a mistake and ascribe the story of an *ing* to an *ought*, or vice versa. There are people who work well with *ings*, but are totally incompetent in the realm of *oughts*, and there are great masters of *oughts* who have the opposite problem, and are like little children when it comes to *ings*. There's no doubt that I have a certain gift for *oughts*: first of all, I can see them, and second, I can perform various actions with them, or even create them if I wish. As far as *ings* go, the more they have of *oughts* in them, the easier they are for me to manage. Some *ings* have very little *ought* in them. They say there is a dark sea in which *oughts* can't be born, and I am afraid that one day I'll drown in it.

WHAT'S WHAT

The Beastie and the Costume Designer

He'll show you what's what—he'll show you Kuzka's mom!
—D.G.

Who's ever seen *what's what*, a.k.a., as we say in Russian, "Kuzka's mom"? Well, some people have, and some haven't. One little beastie was shown *what's what* so often that the little beastie learned all too well what Kuzka's mom looks like. She doesn't look too good, obviously. Leaves much to be desired, let's say.

Whenever the poor little beastie fell in love, the object of her affections began by courting her, acting sweet and warm. But the day inevitably came when he would tell her, "You dumb beastie, look here,"—and whip out Kuzka's mom. The little beastie was extremely traumatized.

Once, a costume designer began courting the little beastie. Every day he brought a little bowl of wine to her burrow; he bought the two of them tickets to travel to different countries; he groomed her fur. The beastie trusted him, and he brought her to live with him.

The designer said to the little beastie, "In my apartment you can do whatever you like. If you want to use my computer, feel free; if you want to take a bath or use the kitchen to cook, go right ahead. Here's the key to the front door and the fob for the building, and here's a little key for that wardrobe over there. Don't ever open it."

Once, while the designer was sleeping, the dumb beastie took the little key and went to the wardrobe. He probably keeps evening gowns in there, she thought, but I won't mess them up, I just want to take a quick peek. The beastie opened the wardrobe, and there really were gowns in there, too beautiful for words. Some of them shone like the bright star Antares and others were iridescent like interstellar clouds.

The beastie tried on all the gowns, and then she noticed, in the depths of the wardrobe, behind the hangers, a bundled package. She unwrapped it, and inside she discovered—Kuzka's mom. The beastie froze and stared for a long time at the awfully familiar face. Then she rewrapped the package, shut the wardrobe, and got the hell out of there.

EVERY BEAR HAS ITS DAY

There once lived a bear who was always making a mess of things. The bear would pick pinecones in the forest and lose them immediately, discover little treats beneath bushes and in the hollows of trees, and lose those, too. He found mushrooms and pots of honey and borscht, hid them away, and forgot where he had put them. He had paws like a sieve: he'd try to carry water from the Smorodinka River and spill all of it. Bringing cloudberries to his cubs, he'd accidentally eat the bunch along the way. He was carrying his mate once and lost her somewhere in the forests of Bryansk. And his cubs, too, fell from his paws and scattered, like the stars along the Milky Way, in the forests of eastern Siberia. In the forests of the north, he lost the star that Ursa Major had given him for his birthday. At the edge of the woods, he lost his bole and the balalaika he'd played. He lost the fox and the wolf, and the wonder-working icon depicting the Bear God, which had been revealed to him in an enormous tree stump, and he began to lament all his losses in the middle of the world's great forest, every tree of which he had squandered: the birch, the pine, the spruce, and the crabapple.

"O, my pinecones, my treats, my honey and my borscht, my water from the Smorodinka, my cloudberries, my mate and our cubs, my star, the bole and the balalaika, the fox and the wolf, the icon of the Bear God, and every tree that grows in the forest—all the things I've been given, I let them all go," wept the bear. He wanted all these gifts and wonders to be his forever, but they disappeared as soon as he found them, because he was a clumsy bear with paws like a sieve, and couldn't hold on to anything.

Then the Bear God took pity on the bear and took away his memory, so the bear began to forget all the things he'd found as soon as he lost them. He found a pot of honey, lost it, and had no idea the pot was ever there. He met a new lady bear, fell in love, dropped her, and could not recall that he had ever been in love, or that the lady bear had even existed. He encountered a plenitude of gifts and wonders, lost them all, and forgot about them on the spot. And so the bear no longer knew loss, but instead, time and time again, possessed the great joy of discovery.

Sometimes the bear still wept in the middle of the woods, because he had the distinct feeling that he'd forgotten something very important, and this vexed him. But rays of light played along his fur, mushrooms sprouted up after a light rain, pots of honey and borscht materialized in the forest groves, new hollows revealed tasty new treats, new cloudberries ripened, new lady bears appeared on the scene and birthed new cubs, fresh constellations scattered stars down upon him, new icons were revealed to him on new stumps, and new trees grew in the forest of the world. All in all, the bear was rarely bored, and only sometimes, in the middle of a sunny afternoon, for a moment, a sense of longing came over him—a longing for something he couldn't remember. But such moments didn't last, and the bear's day went on, full of wonders and discoveries, senseless and everlasting.

THE BEASTIE'S TEARS

There once was a little beastie who cried and cried. She sat there in a pool of her own tears and kept on crying. Everyone fell all over themselves trying to console her.

"What a good beastie!"

"Such a cute beastie!"

"You're the best beastie in the world!"

"It will all work out and they'll get married!"

"God is innocent and we have free will!"

"What's real is rational, and what's rational is real!"

But the beastie still cried and cried.

"Don't cry, you dumb beastie, everyone's going to die anyway," said a mole.

For some reason this worked. The beastie wiped away her tears and began gnawing dry needles and little bugs out of her fur.

THE TALE OF ANOTHER SILLY LITTLE BEASTIE

From the Great Chronicle of the Sufferings of Silly Little Beasties, kept by the fallen angel Turiel since the beginning of the world

I. There was a certain silly little beastie who was not fit for any kind of work.

II. She could not do intellectual work, because she was very stupid. Neither could she do physical work, because she was very weak. Going to an office five days a week was also not an option for the beastie, because she just couldn't be bothered.

III. But the little beastie needed to feed herself, and she had nothing to eat.

IV. Then the little beastie understood that she could only work as biological raw material.

V. At first she gave blood, but this earned her very little money, so the little beastie began to participate in trials of new pharmaceuticals. She was given pills and shots and then observed to see what would happen to her. What happened to the little beastie were very bad things, but there was nothing to be done about that.

VI.   Then the little beastie began to sell her eggs.

VII.   Then the little beastie had an embryo sewn into her belly and became a surrogate mother.

VIII.   And then the little beastie sold her little tail, her little ears, her paws, her liver, her kidneys, and her heart, and donated her skeleton to science.

IX.   Nothing remained of the silly little beastie.

X.   But a few people received transfusions of the little beastie's blood, and this kept them alive, and others were saved by her liver, kidneys, and heart; the child that the little beastie bore grew up to be a good person, as did the children who were created using the little beastie's eggs. The new pharmaceuticals that had been tested on the little beastie advanced medical science and also saved the lives of many people.

XI.   And later still, students learned anatomy using the little beastie's skeleton. And even if this skeleton was not particularly helpful to them in their studies, students being a generally dim bunch, then at least it was good for a few laughs, since every time the lecturer took the little beastie's skeleton out of the cabinet, the auditorium filled with laughter—a laughter heard since the beginning of the world, as people laugh at the shame and suffering of the flesh—involuntary, helpless laughter, mixed with fear.

IN MEMORY OF THE BLACK RHINOCEROS

The sun reaches its zenith and seawater evaporates and returns as rain. Tussocks of grass with tough, narrow blades are scattered across the savannah, shrubs sprout fresh leaves, the flowers of the rainy season blossom. The black rhino tugs at young shoots of grass with his upper lip. The last of his kind, he's slow-moving, mournful. His head bears two horns, which are targeted by hunters, though they're completely useless. The rhino doesn't know that myths and superstitions about horns have caused the extinction of his kind. He barely remembers other large animals like himself; only with some deep animal memory does he recall his mother. For the first two years of his life, he followed her and drank her milk. Then his mother collapsed in a black-gray leathery heap on the grass near their watering place. The rhino nudged her, tried to get her to rise, but she didn't get up, and he went on to wander alone. The rhino has a single friend—a little bird with a red beak who lives on his back and pecks at the ticks that feed on him. During the day the rhino and the little bird journey across the savannah, and when the rhino sleeps, folding his legs and resting his head on the ground, the little bird goes to sleep on his back. The rain comes down in a flood, a true tropical storm; the last black rhino and the red-beaked bird, sheltering beneath a tree, look out at the expanse of the savannah, lashed by countless streams, and carry on their leisurely conversation.

THE GIRL AND THE MOTH

There once was a girl who befriended a moth. She didn't have any human friends and wasn't allowed to keep pets, so she bonded with the moth that lived in the wardrobe. The girl would open the door of the wardrobe and talk to the moth, while homely butterflies the color of dusty moonlight and saber-toothed caterpillars went on mutely devouring the wool, leather, fur, and other textiles and materials.

THE DOG

There once lived a little girl who liked to hang out in empty lots at night. She had no friends and her parents didn't understand her, so she spent her days sleeping and her nights wandering around. This little girl was actually not that little, she was about seventeen. Walking through empty lots alone at night, she felt a sense of longing for a great destiny. She wasn't sure what she was destined for, but she longed for whatever it was with all her heart. Her soul was melancholy and racked with pain, and she always dressed in black.

One cool, dark July night, the girl let down her long black hair and went wandering in a lot by Novoizmailovsky Prospekt, near her house. The lot wasn't large, but it had charm. There were beer cans and car tires, used condoms, a few syringes, and a little black pond full of duckweed, slimy and disgusting, like the seed of some masturbating demon. The girl pissed in the weeds by the pond, then went to look at the water. She wanted to see her reflection, the image of a mystical princess, mistress of abandoned lots and the blighted urban landscape. After all, every landscape needs and nurtures its proper master, from the Erlking to the Butcher of Rostov.

And so the girl peered into the pond—and saw a rib cage. The rib cage stuck out slightly above the water, bits of decaying flesh clinging to the bones. The girl contemplated. She snapped off a long aspen twig and poked at the bones. She lifted some of the gunk that had collected on the rib cage and tried to tow the ribs toward the shore. The rib cage did not budge. The girl wasn't strong enough. "But there are probably people looking for him," she thought, "they've probably long declared him missing. They called around all the hospitals and morgues and couldn't find him." The girl felt sorry for the rib cage's relatives. "I could leave," she thought, "I could go home and forget all about it. I could go on living like none of this ever happened. But he'll stay here, unburied, not at rest, these murky waters his final refuge. Most likely he was murdered and tossed into the pond by his killers to get rid of the body." The girl decided to show some integrity and retrieve the corpse, no matter what.

She went out onto the avenue and stood by the intersection for a while, looking carefully at the occasional drunken passersby. Finally, a pale-haired, stumbling little man with a blue-tinged face satisfied her requirements.

"Come with me," said the girl.

"To where?" asked the man, astonished.

"To that abandoned lot."

"What for?"

"There's a body," the girl explained. "He drowned, I can't get him out by myself."

The man came with her, but he had such trouble walking that the girl was forced to take him by the arm. They reached the pond.

The rib cage was where she'd left it. Little by little, with the aid of a huge broken branch, the man managed to tow the rib cage to the shore. Along with the rib cage, the entire skeleton became visible. It was the skeleton of a large dog.

"Lady, why did you make me do that?" the man asked. "What, were you just curious?"

"No," said the girl, "I wanted to help. Now leave."

The little man looked at the girl in bewilderment, wondering whether it was worth asking if she was up for what he had in mind. The girl, in her long black dress, with her loose black hair, stood regally in the light of the cratered moon, among crooked trees and wilting bushes. The little man understood that she called the shots around here and didn't dare. Stumbling, he made his way back toward the streets.

The girl sat down by the edge of the pond. She composed a simple prayer for the dog's soul. "God, grant the dead dog peace, let it rest easy," the girl murmured. Then she walked home and went to sleep; it was almost dawn.

The girl dreamed of a huge white dog. The dog looked at her with grateful human eyes, then wagged its tail and ran off along a flowery hillside. Above the hill arched a large, glimmering rainbow made up of a million varicolored floating droplets, a rainbow so bright that it was strange and difficult to look at it with the poor little eyes of a girl who was used to the dark.

I KNOW SOMETHING YOU DON'T KNOW

The little lynx and the bunny rabbit are lying there, they're in love, the bunny is spooning the lynx. The lynx is happy, going purr-purr-purr, and then the bunny asks, "Lynx, why are you smiling so mysteriously, like you know something I don't know?"

"I do know something you don't know, Bunny," says the lynx, "but don't ask me what it is, I'm not telling you."

"Oh, tell me, Lynx, I want to know, too," says the bunny rabbit.

"I do know something, Bunny, but don't ask me what it is. I won't tell you."

Then the bunny rabbit says to the lynx, "If you love me, you'll tell me."

"Fine," says the lynx, "if you really want me to, I will. I know something that every lynx knows, but not a single bunny rabbit does. I know how bunnies taste."

SPRING IN THE
GARDEN OF GEOMETRY

The circle blooms with crimson flowers, the triangle with navy-blue ones, the square with white flowerets. From the young grass, a devil's tuning fork rises—optical illusion, impossible trident, tri-une point. Moebius strips slither like snakes through the greenery, and teenagers chug beer from Klein bottles on the banks of a dodecagon-shaped pond. The flowers grow in refined forms: the petals of one are a pseudosphere, the stem of another is weighed down by a heavy golden superegg. Escher's endless staircase has found a home here, as has Bruegel's gallows crow, the gallows now an impossible object. "The way to the gallows runs through merry meadows"—so let us make merry beneath the canopy of a trapezoidal acacia, stroll in the shade of tetra- and octahedrons, and pay our respects to the figure at the center of this garden, one who has unified point and line, plane and space—the kingly Tetractys.

III

THE TRIALS
OF
IVAN PETROVICH

I saw such faces as I had never seen, and heard such words as I had never heard. What can I say to you? Fearful and awful things had I to see and hear for my sins . . .

—The Trials of Blessed Theodora

1

IVAN PETROVICH AND THE SEXTON

Ivan Petrovich had been going somewhere on the metro, but he got off a commuter train at a remote station in a green wilderness. Slowly, bundle on his back, he wandered on along the tracks until they were lost beneath the sand near a small town square. In a little summery café built out of light wood he bought a cheburek. A church complex peered out from behind the trees.

"Coo-coo!"—a frisky, drunk sexton clambered out from beneath the skirts of a red-faced woman selling scarves, sweets, and wooden combs. With motherly reproach, the woman said to him, "You're always showing off, Venechka."

"Join me for a cold one?" asked the sexton. He and Ivan sat down in the hot sun, and the sexton made his confession.

"I once had a wife, and one day she calls me and says, 'Meet me in the Czech Republic, at the Geese and Granny Hotel, I'll be waiting.' So Slavik and I go there, we search the whole hotel and we can't find her. We go down to the cellar, and in the cellar they have a bar and billiards. Some girls are sitting down there around a table playing cards, and each one is more horrible than the next: one's got no teeth, one's got no eyes, one just plain has a horse's head for a face, and there's a single spot at the table that's empty. And these girls are giggling, chatting, and talking to that empty spot, calling it by my wife's name. And Slavik and I got so scared that we bolted, ran fifteen kilometers without stopping. And the next day my wife died."

"And I," replied Ivan Petrovich, "worked at Moscow State University. One day I'm heading downstairs, and I see my mother and father standing there in the stairwell. I got angry at them, that they won't leave me alone, came to Moscow to bother me, so I shoved my mother, and she turned into a little candle, flew down the stairs, and broke to pieces. And my father also turned into a candle and broke to pieces. I was frightened, I went down and started gathering up the candles, trying to fit the little pieces of wax together. Next thing I know, my parents are standing next to me, sort of separately from the candles. My mother takes her candle into her hands and says: 'We'll all be there.' I get home and Aunt Tanya's calling from Osinovaya Roscha to say that our house burned down last night and my parents died."

"Right," the sexton says, "I see. Well, I better get going, wife's waiting."

"Who?" Ivan Petrovich didn't understand.

"My wife," says the sexton. "Look, she's coming over here, looking for me."

Ivan Petrovich looked, and it was true: the sexton's wife was approaching.

2

IVAN PETROVICH, LIAR

Ivan Petrovich was waiting in a long line to enter an administrative building of the Stalinist type; he was supposed to be issued some documents there, most likely a death certificate. There were a couple of freaks waiting next to him: one had wide-flaring nostrils, like a horse, scabs all over her body, and curlers on her head, while the other was dressed up like a little girl, in a very short, pleated skirt that showed off her elephantine, cellulite-ridden legs, and a tank top with a picture of a black bunny, her huge breasts bursting out. There was a revoltingly flirty look on her triple-chinned face. In front of Ivan Petrovich in the line stood a man on all fours. The woman in curlers kicked this man in the ass, and he, thus jolted, rushed to take his place behind Ivan Petrovich—who turned around and realized that the man was none other than his school friend Slavik. Joyfully, they embraced, and, forgetting all about the line, went strolling through the neighborhood of their childhood—through the courtyards by the bay.

The conversation flowed without hurry, like the little winding path past the blue-green kindergarten building, built as though out of toy blocks. They came to the shore of a frozen river, and Ivan Petrovich thought it might be the Smolenka, but this river grew shallow as it ended, and finally flowed into a narrow street.

The street ran into the river, the river into the street, and each was an extension of the other, like an arm and a shoulder.

An ice rink had been set up on the river, and Ivan Petrovich and Slavik decided to skate. Slavik skated freely and easily, and it was as though he had grown younger. Ivan Petrovich, on the other hand, couldn't get the hang of it, as though something heavy and adhesive were clinging to his feet. Meanwhile Slavik skated in circles around him, nagging: "You told Tsypina behind my back that I kissed her friend, Kiselyeva, but I never did anything with Kiselyeva, and Tsypina dumped me."

"What are you talking about?" said Ivan Petrovich—even as he remembered that yes, he had said that, because he'd had a crush on Tsypina himself. "I don't know what you mean," said Ivan Petrovich, "I never told her that."

"Is that so?" said Slavik. "Because Tsypina and Kiselyeva are really beautiful now."

"I wouldn't know," said Ivan Petrovich. "I haven't seen them, it was all so long ago, let's drop it."

"Well, no," said Slavik. "It was just the other day, and you saw Tsypina and Kiselyeva today. Tsypina, you know, is still upset about it."

3

IVAN PETROVICH AND THE BYDLO

Ivan Petrovich was on a train, and sitting across from him was the bydlo. Ivan Petrovich immediately knew the bydlo for what he was—by the track suit, the flat cap, the bloated red face of a gym rat turned alcoholic. The train was passing through the bare white scrim of winter as though tearing through a mourning veil. The bydlo was greedily chomping greasy chicken and washing it down with cheap beer and ardent burping. Once he had had enough, the bydlo felt like chatting, and began glancing over at Ivan Petrovich, who squirmed in his seat and tried not to meet the bydlo's eyes.

"I'm a cultured person," thought Ivan Petrovich, "I don't know this character and I don't want to know him. But I do know a little something about him. He's ripe for a sewage treatment plant, that's what I know about him."

To avoid the bydlo's stare, he pretended to be engrossed in something outside the window—though there, in the drab, dusky gloom, creatures were gathering whose features seemed to be half-face, half-vortex, a visage like Munch's *Scream*, and they pressed in against the glass, clearly wishing to swallow the train with their gaping mouths. Yet the spectral landscape outside— whether sea, sky, or pale frozen flame—through which the train was passing did not faze Ivan Petrovich. What fazed him, rather, was the bydlo. Fazed him and made him indignant. "How dare he?" thought Ivan Petrovich about the bydlo. "How dare he?"

The bydlo eventually did dare, and struck up a conversation in a tone that made Ivan Petrovich's guts seize and nearly gave him nervous diarrhea.

"You do your service here, brother?" asked the bydlo, and for material assurance clapped Ivan Petrovich on the shoulder.

"No, I didn't," Ivan Petrovich forced out.

"All right, you did it over there then," guessed the bydlo. "I see you're a grown-ass man, I'm just a grunt compared to you."

"Grown or not, you've certainly got a few years on me," Ivan Petrovich prepared to say, then noticed his own hands and gasped: he had become an old man of at least eighty.

"You're all right, I can tell," the bydlo continued, more and more heartily, "you oughta live to a hundred. You got an old lady? Listen to me, find yourself a twenty-five-year-old Grandma doesn't know about. Sure, I didn't go to war like you, but I know a thing or two about life. I'm no dummy, right? Isn't that right, I'm no dummy?"

"Right," gulped Ivan Petrovich, "you're not a dummy, certainly not."

"I work security at an elite private school, I'm basically a unofficial cop. Believe it or not, I'm sitting here drinking this beer but there's this one story that seems like it just happened yesterday—" and the bydlo began to tell tale after tale. His reserve of these could not be exhausted, just as his beer somehow could not be exhausted—no matter how much he drank, the bottle stayed full.

"When will this train stop?" thought Ivan Petrovich, and finally, in the break between the twelfth and thirteenth tale, he dashed through the empty train cars toward the driver's compartment. The compartment was unlocked, and when Ivan Petrovich burst in, he saw that there was no driver inside, and nothing else either, no buttons of any kind, no levers. Only a bucket of woodchips, for some reason. Somebody clapped him on the back.

"You're a good old fart," said the bydlo. "We're gonna smoke, and then I'll tell ya another one."

Ivan Petrovich fell feebly against the windshield glass and looked out, into the unknowable reaches of the washed-out, viscous waste. And right away, responding to his gaze, like moths to a flame, the Munchian specter-vortexes began to congregate, pressing against the glass and yawning open the craters of their mouths.

"Look at 'em yappin'," the bydlo marveled, and in an excess of feeling added, "who's my sweeties, who's my little whities."

4

IVAN PETROVICH, FOREIGNER

Ivan Petrovich was walking through the city and eating, out of boredom. He had something at every fast-food restaurant and dive he passed. He ate a crêpe with ham and cheese, he ate a baked potato, he ate a shawarma, a Twister, a sandwich. His boredom grew and grew, just like his belly. Finally, he spotted a stand selling pastries. He was eyeing the pastries when a woman with a double chin ran up to him, saying, "Oh, but sonny, you're a foreigner! You shouldn't eat here."

Ivan Petrovich, so as not to ruin the joke, responded in English: "Yes."

But the lady thought he was saying есть, meaning "eat," or rather not saying, but declaring, imperiously, so she took him to a special café for foreign visitors. Behind the counter at this café stood a different lady, with a triple chin, who winked at him sympathetically. Ivan Petrovich ordered a coffee and potatoes, was brought a pinch of potato peels, and told: "That'll be one hundred and fifty dollars."

"Are you kidding me?" said Ivan Petrovich. "I'm not actually foreign, clearly."

"Oh, you're foreign, we'll show you just how foreign you

are," said the ladies. "And you better pay up, or we're calling the police."

Ivan Petrovich tried to leave, but the women jumped on him like wild tigers. Eventually, with great difficulty, Ivan Petrovich managed to escape, with the ladies crying after him, "Fine, go back to your Congo."

5

IVAN PETROVICH AND THE LONG-AWAITED TRAIN

Ivan Petrovich found himself at N Station, which consisted of a large station building, and next to it, a hotel. Ivan Petrovich headed toward the latter. The hotel turned out to be in mourning. The porter was sobbing, as were the receptionist, the maids, and the long-term guests.

"It actually came!" the receptionist told Ivan Petrovich.

"What came?"

"The train."

"Which train?"

"The long-awaited train!" And then the receptionist told Ivan Petrovich the following.

The entire population of N Station had long been split into two unequal parts. The greater part lived at the hotel and spent all their time there, in idleness or reflection, reading books, organizing philosophical debates, making art—however they pleased. The lesser part of the population lived at the station, because they were afraid of missing the long-awaited train. Those who lived at the hotel thought that no train was ever going to arrive at the station, because although the station had always existed, not a single train had ever pulled in. But those who lived at the station believed that the train would certainly arrive. The hotel-dwellers considered the station-dwellers bums, because who has ever heard of living at a train station?

The station-dwellers also occupied themselves with various things: they sang songs resembling Roma melodies, wrote poems, sketched, and talked with one another, but their art and conversation were fundamentally different from the art and conversation of those who lived at the hotel. You could say that two totally distinct cultures and languages had developed at the hotel and the station. In one language as in the other, people sang songs and wrote poems about the train, and it should be noted that the people who lived at the hotel were certain that they knew much more about the train than those who lived at the station, and that the essential mystery they'd grasped was the mystery of the train's absence. "The train is always with us, it's present in its absence, so it is absolutely unnecessary to go to the station"—thought the people in the hotel. "And these fanatical bums living at the station are simply afraid of this terrible truth about the eternal absence of the train, which is only emphasized by the eternal presence of the station."

"And then yesterday," and here the receptionist began to sob loudly, "there was the sound of a loud horn. You could hear it throughout the hotel, and all the long-term guests ran to the windows that face the station, and from the windows and the balconies they watched through their binoculars as the train approached the station, those who lived there got on, and the train immediately pulled out.

"Some of the people living at the hotel ran headlong to the station, to catch the train—but it was useless, not one of them made it in time. Some hotel-dwellers committed suicide. Some convinced themselves and others that the train had been a mass hallucination. And some went to live at the station, hoping that one day the train will come again. The strangest thing," the receptionist glanced around and whispered in Ivan Petrovich's ear, "is that the director of the hotel, the renowned intellectual and gifted poet Mr. Kryzhovin, author of three poetry collections dedicated to the long-awaited train, was at the station when the train arrived. He went there occasionally to study the lives of the people there, for the purpose of writing an academic work. He could have boarded the train. He was standing right on the platform when it came. He watched the train's arrival and departure, and then returned to the hotel, and hasn't said a word about it.

"And so that's that," said the receptionist. "It actually came. Now, which do you want? Will you take a room at the hotel, or go to the station and wait—maybe someday the train will return?"

Ivan Petrovich pondered, scratching his pate. "All right, give me a room, preferably a luxury suite," he said finally.

6

IVAN PETROVICH AND THE GHASTLY HAND

Ivan Petrovich found himself inside a shadowy building. He was surrounded by people whose faces were concealed by hoods. In the center of the space stood an altar, on which lay a sacred book. Ivan Petrovich approached the book and saw that it was his doctoral dissertation.

"Thief, thief," the hooded crowd hissed at Ivan Petrovich. "You stole my idea, my style, my paragraph, my chapter!"

"All right, I stole them," Ivan Petrovich attempted to defend himself, "but all of you stole, too. What, did you write your dissertations yourselves? Nobody does that!"

"Thief, thief," hissed all these countless philologists, literary scholars, full professors, and authors of articles and monographs whom Ivan Petrovich had robbed. Knowing instinctively what he had to do, Ivan Petrovich grabbed the sacred dissertation and flung it into the circle of people closing in on him. Forgetting all about Ivan Petrovich, the hooded throng ferociously tore the book to pieces as they fought over it, and, having yanked away their individual little scraps, all began to write something on the basis of these.

Not five minutes hence, some had a finished article, others a dissertation, still others an entire monograph. Humbly and deferentially, they approached a heavy iron door with a sign saying

Publication, and formed a line. Periodically the door would open slightly, and from behind it emerged a twisted, cadaverous hand with long, talonlike fingernails, and snatched the papers from their trembling grasp.

As this occurred, some of the hooded figures fainted, their hoods fell away from their faces, and it became clear that they had no faces at all, but rather pages of letters shifting without cease, arranging themselves into citations of some sort only to break apart again and form different citations. The biggest smart-asses had letters that would now and then line up to form preachy quotations from the classics—the more accessible classics, anyway—and their citations were a little thin. Others had letters that kept trying to form four-letter words. It apparently required no little effort to keep this from happening—roughly the same kind of effort it takes to control your facial expression. This was most likely why they had to wear the hoods.

Sometime after the twisted hand had taken the texts away, it tossed them back out, and it became evident from the state of the paper that there, behind the door, the texts had been used to wipe someone's ass. For the hooded academics this was simultaneously the greatest happiness and the utmost torment. Every single one of them, bursting with self-importance, awaited the moment when his text would, at long last, be used as an ass-wipe. Ivan Petrovich also got in line, with an article he had just copied from one of his colleagues. The closer his turn drew, the humbler he felt. Finally, directly in front of him, from behind the door, came the twisted hand with its talon-like nails. Before plucking the papers from Ivan Petrovich's grasp, it ran its fingertips over his face, as though palpating it, and paused for a moment by his lips. Ivan Petrovich kissed the hand and fainted.

7

HOW THEY STOLE IVAN PETROVICH'S WIFE

Ivan Petrovich was walking with his wife Masha through an enormous shopping mall, and Masha was nagging him: "Buy me a fur coat, buy me a fur coat."

"Masha," said Ivan Petrovich, "you're either very stupid or completely shameless, or, most likely, both. You know that I teach, you know how much I make, and you know I have to renovate the dacha—so what are you talking about, Masha? What fur coat?"

"Buy me a fur coat, buy me a fur coat," Masha whined. At that moment, from the Furs for Your Floozies boutique emerged a guy with an elephant trunk and a bottom lip that hung down to his navel. In his arms he cradled a fur coat the color of dark chocolate, with white undertones and a light blue lining.

"Maria, please allow me to present you with this," the man said, and got down on one knee before Masha, offering up the coat. "It's a coat of Barguzin sable, worth seventy thousand dollars."

"Oh!" Masha exclaimed, "it's just what I wanted! Who are you, valiant knight?"

"I am your longtime admirer and cannot live without you. Marry me!"

"Hey, hey, take it easy," Ivan Petrovich cut in. "As a matter of fact, this is my wife."

"You stay out of it, loser, nonentity," said the man with the trunk. "You can't even make enough money to get your wife a coat, what can you do? And you call yourself a man?"

Ivan Petrovich swung back to punch the boor in his rude elephant mug, but, with a single twitch of his trunk, the man tossed Ivan Petrovich into a wall. Meanwhile, Masha put on the fur coat and took the freak's arm, and the two of them, kissing lustily, headed for the exit.

Ivan Petrovich sat up against the wall, humiliated and shaken. A dwarf with his fly down was passing by; he winked at Ivan Petrovich and said: "Don't be mad, buddy. She was too fine a woman for a miserable loser like you."

8

IVAN PETROVICH AND THE STUDENT PRANK

Ivan Petrovich was sitting in his office in the Russian Literature department, only the department was part of an agricultural college, and the agricultural college was housed in an abandoned factory on the Obvodny Canal. The only students there were the less fortunate: addicts, alcoholics, people with HIV. The college fed all of them, dispensed minimal doses of drugs, provided medical care as best it could, and buried them right there, at a cemetery on the factory grounds.

It so happened that a student, Lykov, came to see Ivan Petrovich to retake an exam.

"Let's hear," said Ivan Petrovich, "about Dostoyevsky."

"Huh? I'm here to retake the gym test."

"Then why are you bothering me?"

"You're, like, the gym teacher here," Lykov said, and started doing jumps. He jumped badly, barely leaving the ground before flopping down again like a frozen chicken. "I can't do anything," he said finally. "I got the shakes."

"Then come in the fall," said Ivan Petrovich.

"But by fall I'll be dead," said Lykov. "Just give me the grade now."

"I can't just give you a grade for nothing."

"Not for nothing—for a thousand dollars," winked Lykov, and took a thousand dollars out of his pocket. Ivan Petrovich's eyebrows shot all the way up, but Lykov said, "Don't be shy, old pal, it's not like I can take it to the grave with me."

Ivan Petrovich gave him a passing grade, but as soon as Lykov had shut the door behind him, the money turned into potato peels. Ivan Petrovich ran to find Lykov and give him a beating, and Lykov was there at the cemetery digging himself a grave with his hands, and the bottom of the pit was strewn with potato peels.

"What's up, boss, looking for more money? Come and get it, all you can carry," Lykov snickered.

Ivan Petrovich only spat on the ground, swore, and plodded back to his office.

9

IVAN PETROVICH ON THE ADMISSIONS PANEL

Ivan Petrovich was staffing the admissions panel of the philology department, administering entrance exams. The panel, consisting of a desk at which Ivan Petrovich sat, was in the underground lobby of the Kuzminki metro station. Applicants arrived on the trains, sat down at the desk, responded to the exam questions, received their scores, and departed.

Before the exam began, some people dressed in black had come to Ivan Petrovich to pass on a list handed down from "up above." The list contained the surnames of people who had to be admitted. Ivan Petrovich didn't know who was on the list because of bribes and who was on it because of family connections, but his job wasn't to think about that, his job was to push some through and flunk the rest.

An applicant sat down at his desk: Zhivotov. For a nose he had an obscene hand gesture, his naked gut was bedecked with gold chains, and his exam response was: "I don't read books, I make dough, and you, asshole, better give me the best grade or I'll bury you." Applicant Zhivotov was on the list, and Ivan Petrovich gave him the highest possible score.

He wiped the sweat from his forehead—and here came Applicant Zobov, responding outstandingly to all the questions.

Even his face was normal, a pleasant sort of face, only he had a bird's gullet, a huge one, but everything else was in order. Ivan Petrovich looked at his list and found that Zobov was not on it. Ivan Petrovich wanted to break the rules and give Zobov a high score anyway, but just as the thought occurred to him, a black-gloved hand appeared in front of his face and wagged its index finger.

"Unfortunately, you did not provide a satisfactory response," Ivan Petrovich said to Zobov, who puffed up and clucked furiously.

"There, are you satisfied?" Ivan Petrovich wailed at the skies, or, rather, at the stone vaults of the station. Then the hand in the black glove appeared again and approvingly pinched Ivan Petrovich's cheek.

10

IVAN PETROVICH AT LYOLIK'S FUNERAL

Ivan Petrovich was waiting for a bus at a remote bus stop in the southwest. Along both sides of the road ran vacant lots, overgrown with wilted, yellowing grass. Next to the stop, a homeless-looking guy strummed a guitar. A bus appeared, and Ivan Petrovich got on it.

"Where're we headed?" he asked the dusty, mustachioed driver in his plaid cap.

"From Zvonkovo to Harlushina, for the revel," the driver replied.

The bus rolled on, and the autumnal wastes suddenly became a spring forest. The driver let Ivan Petrovich out on a green public square where a great multitude of people had gathered. Bonfires burned, and in the middle of the square, before a mighty obelisk, an eternal flame had been lit. This was the funeral of Lyolik, a good friend of Ivan Petrovich's. Lyolik was to be interred in the center of the square, beneath the obelisk, as a reward for his great services to the nation.

Ivan Petrovich had always been secretly jealous of Lyolik's rise at work, which was faster than his own, and he suspected that Lyolik had wanted to curry favor and was not above kissing some ass to do it. And now he was being buried with such pomp that a furious Ivan Petrovich said, vehemently, "You won't get to lie here, damned office drone," and dove into the grave beneath the obelisk himself.

In response, Lyolik hopped out of his coffin and began dragging Ivan Petrovich out of the pit. Meanwhile, the crowd in the square began to grumble.

"Get out of my grave!" shouted Lyolik.

"You can't make me!" Ivan Petrovich yelled in response.

Enraged, the crowd rushed at them, and Ivan Petrovich and Lyolik both leapt out of the grave where they had been lying, holding one another in a stranglehold, and ran like hell for the woods, showering each other with curses as they went.

11

IVAN PETROVICH AND THE RUINED DATE

Ivan Petrovich had a date with a woman he'd met on a dating site, whom he had tried to impress in every possible way. He was great at this and at that, he said, smart as all get-out, well-educated, wealthy, good-looking, gentlemanly, a very deep and totally unique person. He wrote all this on his laptop in the evenings, while his wife Masha was in the kitchen cooking or doing laundry, thinking with a mix of pity and resentment that Ivan Petrovich was on his computer because he was working: pity because he had to work nights, and resentment because no matter how much he worked, he never brought in any more money.

When Yulia, as this woman was called, finally agreed to meet, Ivan Petrovich—perfumed, sans wedding ring—picked up three carnations and headed straight to her house. Yulia lived outside the city, inside a hill at the garbage dump. Ivan Petrovich knocked, and an attractive brunette opened the door. She was wearing a delicate periwinkle robe, which Ivan Petrovich stripped from her in one swoop, pulling her to him. Yulia had three gigantic breasts; she swung the side breasts over her shoulders, so they didn't get in the way, but Ivan Petrovich even found this minor flaw charming. They had tea, chatted a little, and soon wound up in bed, where the unforeseeable occurred—Ivan Petrovich couldn't do it. Though this was not really so unforeseeable, since it had been going for about five years.

"So," said Yulia. "You wrote to me that you were so very remarkable: smart, well-educated, wealthy, good-looking, gentlemanly, a very deep and totally unique person. Here's what I'll say: you seem pretty stupid, you're apparently broke, since you brought me three lousy carnations and you're wearing cheap cologne that smells worse than this garbage dump; there's not a lick of depth or uniqueness in you, and you're a complete caveman based on everything you've said. But the worst thing, Ivan Petrovich, is that you're IMPOTENT!"

"And you, you—" Ivan Petrovich could hardly breathe, "you're a dumb, ignorant, horny bitch, a three-breasted freak, who's going to want someone like you—" and he hit her full-on in the face. Insulted to the depths of his soul, he quickly dressed, went out into the dump, and anxiously lit a cigarette.

12
HOW IVAN PETROVICH WAS ANGERED AT HIS WIFE

Ivan Petrovich was sitting on a stool in an unfinished brick house and staring out the window. Beyond the window lay abandoned fields, vacant lots of dying grass, derelict village houses. He turned and saw that across from him stood a sofa with protruding springs, and on the sofa sat his wife.

Ivan Petrovich sat and stared at her. And his wife sat, one leg crossed over the other, and stared at him. Her left leg was crossed over her right. Ivan Petrovich looked at her and saw that something wasn't right, and rage built within him.

"Why have you crossed your left leg over your right?" he finally asked. "You always sit with the right one crossed over the left."

"I don't know," his wife said. "I just sat down like this."

Ivan Petrovich started shouting at the top of his lungs: "Are you mocking me, Masha? Your right leg is always on top! Why would you sit down this way? You're too dumb to do anything for no reason. And too petty and calculating."

"I don't know," his wife said, "I'm telling you, I just sat down the way it was comfortable," and made an innocent face.

"No, it's not comfortable that way!" roared Ivan Petrovich. He looked at her and saw clearly that her innocence was a façade, that there was cynicism in her eyes. And still she sat saying nothing, just looking at him tauntingly, even rocking her leg a little, doing it on purpose, just to drive him crazy. She makes out like she's such a victim, but in her gaze there's ice-cold malice.

"You're a bitch, Masha, a bitch," Ivan Petrovich said to her, "a real honest bitch."

And she still sat there with her legs crossed, not moving a muscle, and in her enormous, triumphant eyes there was steel and hatred.

13

IVAN PETROVICH AT LYOLIK'S BIRTHDAY PARTY

Ivan Petrovich was attending a dinner held to celebrate his friend Lyolik's forty-fifth birthday. The table had been laid in a deep foundation pit, in which nothing was visible except the dirt walls and the pale sky, a light drizzle falling from somewhere far overhead. Next to Ivan Petrovich sat his wife, watching carefully to make sure he didn't get drunk and jabbing him in the side with her skinny elbow after every shot he took.

"Ivan, it's your turn to make a toast," said Ksyusha, Lyolik's wife, a woman Ivan Petrovich had been in love with in his student years.

"Lyolik," Ivan Petrovich began, "you're my best friend, one could say my only friend, and I don't know anyone as kind and open-hearted as you are. We've been friends since our school days, and there's not a word I can say against you. You always helped me out when I was in trouble, you stood by me when I needed your support. You were always our pride and joy—first of our class, then of the whole university. No, there's not a word I can say . . . except maybe this, and it's really nothing, Lyolik, it's nothing, it's only that during the government exams you didn't let me copy, and I scored lower than you, Lyolik, even though I always let you cheat off me on exams, remember, Lyolik? And how did you repay me? With the vilest ingratitude—that's what that was, vilest ingratitude. And also—another nothing, Lyolik, a really minor thing—then you made a whole career, rising to head of our department—do you think you did that yourself? Your daddy the great scholar helped you out. How could you have gotten anywhere on your own? I've known you for so many years—believe me, Lyolik, you're not capable of doing anything yourself! And it was supposed to be me, Lyolik, Sergei Yefimovich had me picked out for that job, but you—I know what you did. You came to see Sergei Yefimovich then, you had a talk with him, what did you tell him about me? I know what you said—that I wouldn't manage, that I'm not the right sort of person, that's what you told him! And you told him that your daddy wanted to have a chat with him about you, and they did have a chat, Lyolik, they did. And I fell in love with Ksyusha first, I courted her for two years, brought her flowers three times, took her to the movies twice, and then what happened, you showed up, all cool, with your own car, Daddy's little boy . . . and she ate it up. Is that what a friend does, Lyolik? On your part, was that the right thing to do? When you were writing her love letters, calling her every night, when you were strolling in the Park of Culture together, were you thinking about me then? You didn't think about me, Lyolik, you've never had a thought about anyone but yourself. To conclude, you're a piece of shit, Lyolik. Let's drink to that."

Alone, Ivan Petrovich drained his glass.

14

IVAN PETROVICH AND THE BLOODY THEOLOGIAN

Ivan Petrovich was traveling through a merciful, ancient land, passing over plowed, sunlit fields, until he came to a dark, distant corner of that land, where shadows reigned, cast down from the trees like the black wings of thrushes. Abandoned village houses rose from the hills, deserted, glimmering with gemlike motes of dust, draped with spongy sprays of moss that hung down from the silvery larches like the beards of hanged dwarves. The murky, dark mirrors inside the stone circles of wells, the dried-up fountains, the corpses strewn hither and thither—all of this spoke of the deathly, alien beauty of oblivion.

Yes, that's right, corpses, noted the astonished Ivan Petrovich, surveying his surroundings. A few had already decomposed, venomous snakes lay coiled in the ribcages of others, and some still looked somewhat human. It was evident that the corpses had been horribly mutilated and partially dismembered, and their severed limbs, perforated guts, and torn-out hearts suggested events that were strange and difficult to imagine.

Meanwhile, licking a bloody blade, a cheerful, handsome youth emerged from his hiding place and headed straight for Ivan Petrovich.

"Do not be afraid," the young man said to him. "I've

murdered, raped, dismembered, and eaten so many people today that my hunger is sated at least until tomorrow. So, let's have a chat."

Ivan Petrovich pissed and shat himself, but the young man didn't seem to notice, and being in a blissful, talkative mood, took Ivan Petrovich by the arm and led him along a tree-lined alley. Branches intertwined above their heads, and some unseen bird began a beautiful, sorrowful song.

"I'm not some kind of homicidal maniac, like you might think," the young man said to Ivan Petrovich. "I'm not insane. And I'm not alone in this. If you care to know, I'm the son of the sovereign of this happy land, I had an excellent education, at twenty I earned a doctorate in theology, and I've published many monographs and collections of religious hymns. My friends are the cream of the crop, representatives of our society's cultural and spiritual elite—writers, scientists, journalists, doctors, teachers. We're united in our opposition to the existing order. I can tell by your mug that you're not from around here, so I'll begin at the beginning, in order to explain to you why my dear comrades-in-arms and I murder, rape, and dismember men, women, and children. Have you ever heard of the ruined worlds?"

"No," piteously bleated Ivan Petrovich.

"God, before creating the world they call Earth, unknown to me and acknowledged as the best of all possible worlds, where good and evil are in balance, where anger is checked by mercy, and mercy by anger, created three other worlds, where evil, violence, cruelty, and injustice reigned unchallenged. The virtue of his idea lay in this: only in opposition to a reign of cruelty and evil can righteousness and the free choice of goodness come to be.

God created these three worlds expecting the appearance

of righteous men without compare, but these righteous did not appear. A teensy error, ahem . . . you can't have saints in a world where only evil exists, it turns out. So God destroyed these three evil worlds. And after that he created the best of all possible worlds, Earth, where there is much evil and violence, and these make possible the free choice of goodness. But on Earth there is also mercy and love. There may not be that much of them, but they're God's gift to the righteous, so that these righteous can come into being.

So, because there's love and mercy on Earth, its saints are saintly, if you will. It's not quite one hundred percent, God gave them a leg up, so to speak, but thanks to all that evil and violence that will forever oppose them, there's an aspect of free choice in their righteousness. And that's why God hasn't destroyed the Earth. Is all that clear?"

"It's clear," whispered Ivan Petrovich, and pissed himself again.

"And are you a saint, by any chance?"

"No."

"Then look, this is how it works on Earth, for example. Say the ruler of some country is a bloodthirsty ghoul, for instance. Who is it that challenges him? The opposition. The opposition stands up for goodness, justice, democracy, and whatever else. Members of the opposition go to their deaths, they go to prison, all for the truth. And the guarantee of their freely chosen goodness is—what? Right, it's the ghoulish ruler whose existence allows them to go ahead and be righteous.

"All right, so here's what happened next. Satan, the ape of God, heard about the experiment with the three evil worlds and drew some conclusions. Satan created his own world, where good reigned, and also wisdom, justice, love, and mercy. In this world, everyone was a saint, but there was no aspect of freedom to their righteousness, and so true, freely chosen goodness, the only kind that counts in the eyes of God, was impossible. The thought of this gave Satan great joy. But another thought gave him even more joy. Can you guess what I mean?"

"No," replied Ivan Petrovich, and shat himself again.

"What I mean is that in a world where you can't freely choose to be good, you can still freely choose to be evil. So this blessed world created by Satan turned out to be the prefect potential training ground for unprecedentedly great sinners. But really, since in this world there wasn't a modicum of evil, it was so sterile that even sinners didn't come into being—just as saints didn't come into being in the totally evil world. Satan was a little disappointed, but God . . . God, when he found out about our world, was filled with pity, and decided to give us a chance to be saved. He gave it to us in the most paradoxical way. It may look like he played right into Satan's hands, but it's actually the other way around.

"God sent us Him—oh, what should I call Him? The Light, who came into our world to teach us evil, so that with Him, a bit of evil would appear here, and thus give us the chance to freely choose to do evil. But God's secret design was that, since in this way we received the ability to freely choose evil, we would one day be able to freely choose either good *or* evil.

"After all, if we choose evil and great sinners appear among us, then the deeds they do will bring even more evil into our world, and at some point there will be so much of it, that someone—oh, this great, anticipated hour!—will be able to freely choose goodness. And that person will be the first saint, and after that other righteous men and women will come.

"And so it is the will of God that the Light came to teach us evil. He was the first murderer in our world, the first serial killer, the first madman and rapist. He was impossible, yet he appeared, and brought us hope. And many of our best people, the children and grandchildren of decent folks, the pride of this world, are his followers. Every day, we do as much evil and spill as much blood as we can, and we'll teach our children to do the same, and they'll teach their children, so that one day, one day . . . When there are a great many people who have freely chosen evil, so many that the land drowns in suffering, someone unknown to us, someone not yet born, a boy or a girl, child of this Devil-forged world, will for the first time beneath these skies freely choose goodness."

"So why don't you, young man, uh, freely choose goodness?" Ivan Petrovich humbly inquired.

The question made the young man angry. "I see you're completely dense," he yelled, "because I just told you: in this blessed world I can only *freely* wish for evil. Even when I think about the saints to come, I'm not thinking *freely*, because I'm the son of a good person and the grandson of a good person, born into a world where everyone is, by necessity, good. And I too am only good by necessity, and that is dust in the eyes of God. But the Light has come and allowed me to freely choose evil. Listen, you know what? I'm feeling peckish again . . ." and the young man grinned broadly, taking out his blade and licking it, looking with tender amusement at Ivan Petrovich.

15

IVAN PETROVICH AND THE GREAT CELEBRATION

Ivan Petrovich was sitting in a classroom at his school on Vasilyevsky Island. He was a little boy again, though he somehow remembered everything that would happen later: studying at the university in Moscow, his parents moving to the country, the fight with them over the apartment, his marriage, his divorce.

What a bunch of nonsense I wasted my time on, Ivan Petrovich thought, and yawned. Oleg Shepkin, who sat in front of him, had meanwhile leaned over his desk to pass a note to Kiselyeva. Ivan Petrovich didn't miss a thing. He waited for just the right moment and gleefully poked Oleg right in the rear with his compass.

"Moron," said Shepkin, offended. Suddenly everyone looked over at Ivan Petrovich and shouted, "Moron!" in unison, and though Ivan Petrovich couldn't see himself from the side, he felt that something wasn't right. The something that wasn't right was that Ivan Petrovich had grown donkey ears. Instead of a face he had a piggy snout; he had lost his pants; and on his head he wore a cap and bells.

And then Ivan Petrovich became very merry, and he jumped from his seat and began to dance; he even did the squat dance.

His classmates didn't fare any better. The tall ones became giants, the short ones became dwarves. Yulia Tsypina twirled like a top, Olesya Kiselyeva rolled like a wheel. The very clever, nerdy Hvorostov grew a pimply ass in place of his face, and in place of his ass, a scowling, stuck-up professor's face. Chika Chekhalin was pretending to be the principal, Petya Vosmyerkin was pretending to be Brezhnev, and Ivan Petrovich was supposed to be the Patriarch. He was ceremonially inducted into this office with a flick on the nose.

Then two old women entered the classroom—the singing teacher and the history teacher, both pregnant and struggling to drag along their enormous bellies.

"You there, Ivan Petrovich, summon Lenin, it's not a party without him," they said. "To call him you must do the following: draw a circle around yourself with chalk, doodle some horns on Lenin's portrait, and start reading the Party Statute backwards." Ivan Petrovich got to the reading part and there was Lenin, climbing out of his portrait, horns and all, and breaking into dance.

"Keep reading," said the old ladies, "let them all come out."

Next came Stalin, also with horns, and he started dancing, too. Khrushchev and Brezhnev climbed out, and then people Ivan Petrovich hadn't even heard of when he was in school: Andropov, Chernenko, Gorbachev, Yeltsin, Putin. All had horns, and all were dancing and making merry. And Ivan Petrovich wasn't at school anymore, he was in the Kremlin, and there were thousands of people there with him: civil servants, ministers, mayors, deputies—all of them with horns, all dancing. Ivan Petrovich stood in his chalk circle and wiggled his ass's ears; on his head he wore the fool's cap, on his chest he wore the Patriarchal Cross, and he understood that it was he who had called all of them forth, they were all a part of him, part of his body and his soul, and his country, and his cosmos, and he shouted to them, "Begone!" with all the strength of his piggy snout.

16

IVAN PETROVICH AND THE BABE

Ivan Petrovich was standing in a crowded metro car, and a woman
stood near him with her back turned. Ivan Petrovich glanced at
her and saw that everything about her was just right: she was slim,
her skirt was shorter than short and hugged her tight butt, she
wore heels, and the dragon printed on her tights twined around
her legs. Her hair was curly and red and floated around her head
like a cloud. Ivan Petrovich decided, as usual, to have a little fun.
He leaned toward the woman's musky, fragrant hair, breathed
heavily through his nose right by her ear, and put his sweaty little hand on her ass, starting to carefully feel up her ass and hips.
Suddenly he heard the woman let out a kind of horse whinny. Ivan
Petrovich grew wary, and then the woman turned to face him, and
he saw that her face was covered in dragon scales, her nose was
sunken like a syphilitic's, and on her chin sprouted a bushy red
beard. Ivan Petrovich yanked back his hand, his mouth dropping
open in horror, and the woman bent toward him and whispered
into his ear, "What a bad boy you are, Ivan Petrovich."

17

IVAN PETROVICH HOLDS EXAMS AT THE MORGUE

Ivan Petrovich found himself at the Russian Literature department once more, but this time the department was in a morgue, and his student Shlyutskaya was there to take a final. She showed up in a white sheet, and it was pretty clear—she wasn't even cold yet. She started in on him right away: "I don't know anything about your subject and I don't want to know."

"What are we going to do with you?"

"I'm going to blow you, and you're going to pass me."

"Excuse me, young lady, but you're dead!"

"So, according to you, I'm supposed to know your subject even though I'm dead, but because I'm dead I can't blow you?"

"All right, young lady, but there can't be anything between us, if only because you're my student!"

"Look how righteous you suddenly turned out to be. Masha said it's all the same to you whether a person is alive or dead, a student or not a student."

"Who's this Masha?"

"Your wife Masha, she's here too," Shlyutskaya said. "She says you killed her yesterday. She also says you ruined her entire life and wouldn't buy her a fur coat."

"She's dead and still running her mouth about the coat,

the whore," swore Ivan Petrovich. He gave Shlyutskaya a passing grade and walked out of the department, slamming the door. "You'll see that coat like you can see your own ears!" he bellowed, walking past the freezers.

18

IVAN PETROVICH AND THE BAD HABIT

A man in boxer shorts shot out of the doorway of an old Leningrad apartment building, shouted to Ivan Petrovich, "Watch out, man, it's really something in there!" and ran off.

Cautiously, Ivan Petrovich opened the door—there was a mousehole behind it, and he began to squeeze himself through. After a while the hole became a glass corridor, a sort of subterranean avenue. At intervals, white park benches stood along the walls of the corridor, and on these benches couples sat kissing: men and men, women and women, adults and youths. Ivan Petrovich looked at them askance and kept going. Finally, he entered a gigantic lecture hall. The hall was full of freaks, and upon seeing Ivan Petrovich they broke into loud applause, gesturing to show him that he should ascend to the podium. Ivan Petrovich started to retreat, and tried to run for it, but a sturdy pair of freaks took him by the arms and brought him to the stage.

"Give us a speech," they said. "We're all here thanks to you."

Members of the audience began raising their hands and asking Ivan Petrovich some delicate questions. Did he at some point have a bad habit of so-called self-abuse, and how often did this occur, and in what circumstances? Ivan Petrovich reluctantly admitted that yes, this did happen sometimes, by and large almost every day, in all kinds of circumstances, but mostly in the bathroom.

Following his responses, a woman from the audience brought Ivan Petrovich flowers. She had a harelip, a split chin, and three nostrils, and she said, "Ivan Petrovich, you are our father. Each time you did this deed one of us was born, without a mother, from your seed and the filth adrift in the air. You gave us life, and for that we're going to exalt and adore you."

"You shouldn't, let's not," said Ivan Petrovich, but the freaks were already rising from their seats and encircling him. Just when they'd drawn close and were about to seize him, Ivan Petrovich jumped very, very high, up to the very ceiling, and in the ceiling there was a hole, and the hole sucked in Ivan Petrovich like a vacuum cleaner. But the monstrous creatures had grabbed him by the cuffs of his pants, and the pants remained in their hands, while Ivan Petrovich shot out in just his boxer shorts, saw a door, ran through it into a courtyard, screamed to the puny little man he saw on the other side, "Watch out, man, it's really something in there!" and ran off.

19

IVAN PETROVICH STATES HIS CONVICTIONS

Ivan Petrovich was being interrogated. The investigator, who had introduced himself as a Jesuit priest, shone a light in his face and inquired: "To which faith do you belong, Ivan Petrovich?"

"I'm an Orthodox Christian," said Ivan Petrovich with a gulp.

"Answer all questions honestly," the investigator warned him, "it's your only chance. How would you describe the nature of God?"

"I think God is the lifeforce within all natural things, and the moral law inside me," replied Ivan Petrovich, with a sense of his own accomplishment.

"How wonderfully put," said the investigator. "And do you go to church?"

"Yes, I do," said Ivan Petrovich, "on Easter."

"And how would you describe Jesus Christ?"

"I think he was a wise man, like Buddha, Laozi, and Socrates, and he taught people to do good."

"On the whole, I am satisfied with your answers," said the investigator, "you're an Orthodox Christian, you go to church, you have some wise thoughts about God and Jesus Christ, everything seems to be in order. Do you believe in God, though, if we're being honest?"

"No," said Ivan Petrovich, "probably I don't, I'm a rational person, a man of science, I think it's all a myth people invented to make it less scary to die."

"I see you're no dummy, Ivan Petrovich," said the investigator. "There's no getting one over on you. Since no violations came to light in the course of this conversation, I'll see you at the final judgement."

20

IVAN PETROVICH GETS CAUGHT IN THE STORM

"Hey, you, don't move," a hunchback shouted to Ivan Petrovich from about thirty steps away. Between Ivan Petrovich and the hunchback stood a learning-disabled boy, about equidistant from each of them. Ivan Petrovich froze.

"See, there's a storm now," the hunchback shouted to him between gusts of wind that tugged at his beard. "We can't move, or that boy will die."

While Ivan Petrovich, the boy, and the hunchback stood still, bolts of lightning came ceaselessly from the sky. When the lightning struck the ground, it became enormous chunks of ice, which rolled toward the boy, but stopped just short of him.

Ivan Petrovich noticed, on a nearby mountain, a toy black forest, bristling all over with little plastic trees. Inside the forest were all kinds of enticing wonders: bonfires, campsites, colorful glowing stones. Ivan Petrovich wanted to go into those woods, and took a step toward them. A bolt of lightning immediately hit the boy, and he fell down dead.

"What's the matter with you?" The hunchback ran up to Ivan Petrovich. "Didn't I tell you not to move? We were supposed to stand on either side of him, symmetrically!"

Ivan Petrovich shrugged. "At least spare a dime, for Christ's sake," said the hunchback pitifully.

"Bite me," said Ivan Petrovich, and left. The storm ended.

On the other side of the woods, Ivan Petrovich discovered a ditch filled with sticky gray mud. From this mud, he began to sculpt a horse. He made three versions, but not one of them was right, so he tossed them aside. The unfinished horses took on the form of female creatures with metal cylinders for heads, and began chasing after Ivan Petrovich, who ran from them for a long time through plastic trees and little houses made out of clay.

IVAN PETROVICH AND THE FINAL DECISION

Ivan Petrovich was brought into the courtroom. It was a room of immeasurable size, filled with thousands, maybe tens of thousands of people, but Ivan Petrovich saw many familiar faces among them. The tipsy sexton was winking at him slyly, sitting with his wife in the third row, and Ivan Petrovich even thought he heard: "When it's all over, buddy, we'll have a cold one, I saved some." Lyolik sat next to Ksyusha; Slavik between Tsypina and Kiselyeva. The bydlo sat there in his track suit and cap, eating chicken and drinking beer, burping and chomping. The two pregnant teacher-crones gazed at him with grave accusation. All his school and university classmates were present, too. The VIP seats were filled by all the horned leaders and presidents, from Lenin to Putin, and around them sat civil servants, ministers, mayors, deputies. Ivan Petrovich saw the hunchback, the disabled boy, and the women with metal cylinders for heads. He saw his academic brethren: the countless philologists, literary scholars, full professors with citations where their faces ought to be. He saw Masha in her coat of Barguzin sable kissing the man with the elephant trunk. He saw his students: Lykov in the potato peels, dead Shlyutskaya in her white sheet, bloated Zhivotov, and gullety Zobov. He saw the handsome and happy bloody theologian, licking his blade. He saw the multitude of freaks he had engendered, the woman with the harelip, split chin, and three nostrils, and the babe in the miniskirt with the red hair, scaly dragon-face, collapsed nose, and bushy red beard. He saw three-breasted Yulia in her periwinkle robe and the Jesuit investigator smiling at him. There was neither lawyer nor judge at these proceedings, only a plaintiff with the face of a rooster and a rooster's coxcomb, shouting in a shrill falsetto, "Guilty, guilty!" as the gallery applauded him and called to Ivan Petrovich, "Ours, ours!"

And then there was nothing but a dark empty room in a wooden house, a cracked door letting dim light come through, creaking floorboards, and a bucket of woodchips on the floor.

IV

ἐκπύρωσις

TWO LOVERS LOOK
INTO THE DARK

Two lovers look into the dark, the cold beams of light meeting and parting, the intersections and lines. This is Hiro Yamagata's laser light show above the Neva in 2003, the tricentennial of the city's founding. Blue and green rays cross in the sky, though not in the pale, blue-gray sky of May, but another, otherworldly sky, empty and without limit or end, the black sky of shamans who send forth misfortunes; a sky in which some celestial peril, far worse than the subterranean kind, is always looming.

There is neither earth nor water nor fire, only darkness scored with lines of light. *He lies in a dale of Dagestan among yellow peaks, and a ray of light streams down, and within the ray is a dream, and within the dream is an evening feast in his native land and a young woman asleep, dreaming of a dale in Dagestan.* The lovers are still very young; they were sleeping in each other's arms, but now they're awake and gaze out into the dark. They stare guilelessly, like beasts, with no thought of the future, only vaguely conscious of some threat that in their simplicity they barely notice, gazing forward as though blindly. Mighty and powerful they are before the dark, crowned with the golden crowns of the tsar and the tsaritsa, invulnerable for a while in their crystal citadel. Within the citadel, a flame burns inside a crystal flower, just like in Great-Grandmother's chandelier, and darkness can only lap at the citadel's walls, extruding danger and some indefinite dread, a miasma that seeps through extremely fine cracks in the crystal. For the time being, he still has King Arthur's sword and can slay any creature of darkness that dares approach her. For the time being, there's still an impassable threshold of pure flame, kindled in the crevices of the blaze-black sky.

For the lovers, the darkness is still more like a movie, a thriller playing out on the other side of a glass screen. The vague danger gathers and takes shape; forms and creatures float out from the shadows and and fog up the screen with their breath, licking at the citadel's unbreachable walls with slippery tongues. Serpents' tails appear, and the enormous tentacles of the world's laws, the laws of human nature, which belongs to the dark. In the voices of their mothers, grandmothers, great-grandmothers, dead ancestors unto the seventh generation, the darkness proclaims that the celestial flame will weaken, until one day the onslaught of the dark will prove stronger, and the crystal citadel will shatter into a million shards.

Winds howl in the darkness, and their names are Pain, Sorrow, and Despair. Out of the darkness emerge the stumbling, crooked, hunched allegories of suffering, figures of dissolution and disappointment. Fanning out like a cluster of overripe bananas on a counter are the faces of psychiatrists, packets of prescription drugs, hideous masks of madness. Born from the darkness are the mysteriously attractive, still-unfamiliar faces of other, future lovers.

Like the little red flower from the fairy tale, the most beautiful flower in all the world, the crystal citadel exists only for an instant, standing in opposition to the law. The darkness waits patiently, settling softly around the citadel like a heavy blanket. The defeat of love by the dark.

KARELIA

Late August, the Ladoga Skerries

There's no one else here, neither people nor cars, only Serdobol left behind us. Its name is both silver and bitter; how does anyone live in a place like that, surrounded by silver pines, on a lake cut into by skerries like Norwegian fjords, in a little town like a pendant at the end of a young girl's necklace, with such a name—Serdobol, meaning *heartache*?

Sloping, rounded boulders descend into the water, but they're rough enough to grip with equally rough heels, exposing yourself to the invisible wind, which doesn't even rustle the blue leaves. Best of all is to undress completely and gaze outward, becoming a titan on a stone, a stone carving on the shores of Lake Ladoga, blown clean through with a premonition of autumn, turning translucent, peach-pink at sunset. To sit on the stones like the Little Mermaid statue in Copenhagen, looking over your shoulder at the smooth, calmly plashing water.

Farther, on nearby shores, the forest dips and swells, as

though growing on rounded stone plates that curve up like the shells of giant prehistoric turtles, or the skulls of giants who once scattered these Karelian boulders. It's a wild, petrified place, overgrown with verdure—pines and firs, in which all kinds of birds and beasts have come to live.

Vottovaara, Death Mountain

The closer to the center of Karelia, the denser the taiga: settlements, villages, lakes. Uksuyarvi, Suoyarvi, Porosozero, Gimoly . . .

We ascend Death Mountain at dusk, so that at the summit, by the crater of the ancient volcano, we can look down through a frenzy of pines and catch the last rays of falling light. After that, the return—in total darkness, almost by feel, parting branches, lost without a trail.

In the dark the forest is gray, dense with firs. It has a frightening, spectral beauty. The lower branches of the firs hang down as though swathed in spiderwebs, bowing beneath their own weight. It's not earth you're walking on but boulders, covered in moss deep and smooth as a voice. There's green, downy moss, like a wolfskin or bearskin tossed over the stones. There's reindeer moss, too.

Among the moss and scree, another kind of carpet unfurls— enormous bilberries and cowberries, untouched by human hand. The berries are the size of a thumbnail, sweet, shining brightly along the entire slope, black and crimson. In the dusk, everything glows with richly saturated colors: crimson, emerald, black. The prismatic stones: veins of green, light blue, white. As though they were the bones of some mountain dragon—marble, jasper, malachite.

Standing upright, lean back just a little and you're falling backward onto the soft, berry-oozing, aromatic, mossy, damp slope; falling into some forgotten tale, dark forest lore. And everything entices you to fall and become one with the earth and grass, the hearty trunks and heavy branches. Your eyes already seem to have a special glow. That's the elements entering into you, a boundless stream, night whispers.

Last Night of August, at the Swamp

There's neither lakeshore nor field nearby, so we spend the night at the very edge of a swamp. The forest here is squat, snarled, and squelching—soon enough we find a boggy brown glade, yellow grass and tussocks growing scruffy and irregular, like the bumpy chin of some redheaded imbecile adolescent, in his eyes a look of watery degeneration.

A solitary tree, dead, branches gone, just rough stumps remaining, towers above the grass—naked, but also bearded, somehow. The farther into the wilderness, the nobler the forest becomes, but the closer to the swamp, the more it bristles with cross-eyed stares, crooked smirks, broad gaps between teeth, something in it of an alcoholic, a forest sprite, a minor demon. The swamp is the forest going to pot.

In the morning, the swamp refuses to let us go—our car is stuck. We don't have a winch, only jacks. For a long time I scramble in the rain between the swamp and the road, looking for planks and stones to wedge beneath the wheel. The car groans, struggles, and finally drives on, through the Karelian taiga, twenty or thirty kilometers to the nearest village.

First Day of September, Kayaking on Lake Yudozero

Everything here is blue-gray: lake, boat, oars, sweater, sky—all of it washed-out and pale. The gaze glides along, sated, bored, slipping past the shoreline, until—astonishment! A view of impossible beauty—otherworldly, northern, Karelian.

Colorful cliffs jut into the water, angular and jagged, with sparse, solitary pines growing in spots, their trunks scored with furrows. Each individual furrow stands out, catches the eye, demands attention, contains a pattern unique like the feathery patterns of frost.

A patterned tapestry seems to spread over the stones and cliffs, so they're all garlanded with veins, teardrops, silver. The pinkish mist of the fog that hangs above the shore turns everything into a haze, a thaw. Stones seem sprinkled with snow, but it's really reindeer moss. The moss is pink and glistening, maybe not only reindeer but some other varieties of lustrous northern mosses.

Let your eyes go a bit soft and all of this becomes a shimmering, silvery-pink stone mountain with a pinkish-black lake at its foot. No such lake exists, and no such mountain exists. And there are great crimson cowberries growing between those rocks, and no one is ever going to pick them.

An ancient, gigantic pine once grew among the stones at the water's edge. The pine has died, and its trunk is gone, but a coaly, charred, dry, white-fungus-bedecked tangle of roots remains, like the antlers of an enormous deer.

Faced with all of this beauty, its bounty, variety, opalescence, the play of colors, the drops of mist—you can't fix your gaze on any single thing. You're lulled to sleep right on the water by this impossible, glimmering abundance.

Elmus

On Lake Emus there's also a village called Elmus. About fifty plots, some abandoned. The houses aren't crowded together—there's a lot of space and air here, much of the blessed, the forgotten, the unneeded by anyone.

The houses are gray, damp, and slanted, the fences even grayer, damper, more aslant. There aren't many people, and it seems like it would be charming and melancholy to live here; behind the wattle fence by the lake, a thin young rowan tree sways lightly in the wind, and its berries glow. Everything has converged in these berries, too bright for this unlovely village: my past and my future too, gathered here and suddenly far from me.

Some people we meet let us spend the night in a huge house, once painted green, for the price of two hundred rubles: our landlords are Anatoly Aleksandrovich and Nina Mikhailovna. They make beds for us in a room smelling of aged wood and warmth. The house faces the lake, where Anatoly Aleksandrovich catches fish. There's a chapel nearby that he built, a little wooden one, with a window onto the lake. A solitary boat bobs on the surface of the water.

Everything here feels eternal, sorrowful, and singular like that, as though old Mother Truth has suddenly broken through all of our delusions, and now she sits here telling us about herself: "I'm just another old lady, I get by here little by little, putting away a penny or two, and I am the rowan tree, and I am the lake, and I am autumn itself . . ."

She's still muttering something, telling her tale, but you're no longer listening, you're drifting off, filled with the scent of warm wood.

EVERYONE IN EDEN HAS DIED

Everyone in Eden has died.

Dead are the master of all things and the mistress of all earth.

The jasmine blooms, the seedlings of which the master used to receive by mail from other cities, or they had to be cut early in spring, before the buds bloomed, and stored in the snow or the refrigerator.

B. drowned in the bath, boiled to death in the hot water.

The bench by her veranda is heaped with dry branches from the birch tree that was cut down last year.

Even the Scottish Fold cat who loved to sprawl in the woodpile and follow Mama around the house has died.

All that remains is to salute the casket.

The serpent slides through the tall grass.

The grandchildren of the first people bury their elders.

ἐκπύρωσις

Strings and strands of hair catch fire, eyes and eyelashes catch fire, it happens this morning, today, tonight. The canvas of the sky, from crimson to clover—it isn't canvas but Flemish lace, linen yarn stitched up into the air by golden-haired Godelieve in the old city of Bruges. There's a movie about two hitmen in that town, eternally medieval with its stone towers and spires, wooden bridges, chiming clock, town hall, breweries and museums. All of that is burning.

It's different here. Petersburg autumn, sunset kindled over the Admiralty shipyards, or an early dawn with two celestial bodies at once—the moon and the sun. They're both in the sky at this hour: the moon spills down its pale, twilight green glow; over the fields around Pulkovo Airport planes descend slowly, blinking their lights, and a young man and woman drive into those fields, turn off-road, park, take a blow-up mattress and bottle of wine out of their trunk. Meanwhile the sun is already rising, sending forth the dawn, and the world stands bemused by these two luminaries, as though they aren't supposed to be there together, like a divorced couple.

The dissolving dawn dissolves distance, scatters its rays like a spawning fish, and the world floats in them, weightless. The city in the distance floats and steams, and the planes in the sky, the buildings of the observatory in the tall grass, and maybe some butterflies that haven't yet frozen. Above all else, I love that smell—smoke carried on the wind, coal smoke in which you recognize all other smells combined: the scraped knees of childhood, pain and passion, patchouli and oak moss, wormwood and citrus, sand and asphalt, tire rubber, benzine, cut grass and coffee, vanilla and wine. A stinging, relentless, irrevocable smell, a smell that contains all things—the smell of a world perishing in fire.

Like in disaster films, they'll step out of their cars, leave them behind in traffic jams on the major and minor avenues; maybe, following film logic, they'll begin to dance. They'll dance embraced by tongues of flame, they'll spin like dervishes and lash the air with whips of fire. I heard about a woman from Kyiv who never cared about doing anything, not since she was a little girl—not reading, not playing with toys, not thinking, not speaking, not spending time with other people—except spinning like a top around her own axis, like a Sufi. She spun and spun, learned to spin with torches, left Kyiv and went to Goa, and now she spins there. Kyiv burns, and Goa also burns. Millions of fiery dervishes with burning torches spin around their own axes.

Children run out of the schoolhouse onto the terrace, this is better than summer vacation, little whirls of electricity frolic at their sides. Every gesture leaves a fiery trace in the air. How slow to ignite are time, space, motion, and matter. Teenagers climb to the rooftops to watch the world glow. Old man Indyukov, tubercular, lisping and mean, goes out on his balcony too, to spit at the world one last time. The gob comes out precise and crimson with a black wormhole center, like a poppy flower: tobacco and blood.

The planes above Pulkovo are on fire; the moon burns, so does the nearby Gulf of Finland, as though oil had been spilled into it; virgin soil burns, the president burns in the Kremlin. Food—that's fire, baby, water—that's fire, baby—a Black man with dreads on Nevsky Prospekt sings and drums. Earth is fire. Air is fire. On Liteyny Prospekt costumed Indian princesses with bare bellies sing and dance, and Sufis in the deserted Palace Square recite poems about the exultation of the atoms. Cell membranes turn to blistering plasma, cytoplasm turns to flame. LCD displays melt in the running heat.

On fire are conjunction, disjunction, material implication, the sacrifice of meaning in poetry, the incitements of language, the body, and music. All mirrors break, all images are holy. The waterfalls of worlds are born and burn in the chaotic flux of the Universal foam. From now on, there will be no more strong and weak, master and slave, beauty and beast, distillation of being through reason, word and thing, form and content, thought and sign, holy hierarchy, enlightened monarchy, liberal democracy, or anything else. Only the waterfalls of the burning worlds, the cleansing flame, *ekpyrosis*.

V

FAIRY TALES OF THE NORTH

IN THE SIGHT OF ATHENA

Minerval

Colossal as a death camp, the Minerval market stretches along a long, empty strip of beach. The pale waves of the sea slap weakly against the runny mud of the shore, the stunted shrubs, the hummocks of monotonous tundra. For kilometers there are tents and stands, pavilions, fast-food counters where visitors can sample a sausage roll or a shawarma. The winds are always blowing here, the gulls always circling overhead; rounded sea pebbles and tin cans lie underfoot. The market was once called not "Minerval" but "Minerva," and above its old gates, with something of the crypt about them, a stone statue of Pallas Athena stands to this day, in a helmet with images of winged Pegasus and the Sphinx. Her eyes are inlaid with colored stones; at night they glow crimson and blue, and could well lure sailors who have lost their way—but rarely do any ships sail into these latitudes, these desolate lands back of the north wind . . .

They say that someone who does business at this market, someone whose word here is law, didn't like that the market was named for a woman, even if she is a goddess. So they added an "l" to Minerva, or Athena, and the market became Minerval, which means *student*, or *payment for learning*. If you've ever visited the bazaars of the East, with their bounty and luxury and chatter, the buzzing of insects above the fruit, the piled carpets and sweets— Minerval is the absolute antithesis of these. On show there is all the poverty of doomed Hyperborea, the faded, as though milk-stained, eyes of the hawkers, the track-marked youth, the small-time hustlers. Minerval's principal wares are strange and superfluous mechanical contraptions, automatons and their spare parts, machine bits, porn tapes. In some tents, a pale narcotic brew is simmered in cauldrons, concocted from some homely local grass. A skinner might sell you leather or hides, usually mangy and low-quality. All the cats here are black, there are no other kinds, but there are many of these, and they breed like mad.

The market guards are tasked with catching the kittens, collecting them in large bags, and crushing them with their cars against the asphalt. One of the guards, Derviy, tried to save these cats: he caught them and carried them far away, hiding them so that the others wouldn't find them. He brought a few cats home. The kittens grew up affectionate and sweet. When spring came and the tundra began to bloom, Derviy fell in love with a girl of about thirteen, a seller at the market named Naina. She had faded, as though milk-stained, eyes and pale, sun-bleached braids. Derviy kept wandering past her, brought her a bouquet of drab, plain, but delicate tundra flowers. Naina sat, singing a quiet, obscene song, always the same one, and smoking. She sold hunting rifles.

In the evenings, Derviy watched Naina in secret. After the market closed, he saw her watch porn and masturbate in the pavilion; he saw her eat shawarma, saw her let down her long light hair, saw her sweep the floor of the pavilion and occasionally wipe it with a rag, standing on all fours. Late one night, Derviy saw Naina take a rifle and walk toward the shore, where, in a sandy cave by a large garbage dump, Derviy had hidden some kittens. Derviy understood that Naina was going to kill them. She stuck her head into the cave and aimed her rifle. Derviy took out his knife, went to Naina, pulled her head out of the cave by its pale braids, and cut Naina's throat as she beat against him like a fat white gull. Then he took the kittens and went into the tundra, and never came back again.

Naina survived. They stitched up her throat, and only an ugly scar remains, running across her neck. Years have passed since then, and Naina, aged, faded, with milk-bleached eyes, sits at her stand with the rifles, smokes, and sings a quiet, obscene song, always the same one, but with an added verse about a beloved who cut her throat and went into the tundra. She honors him in the last words of the song. Hungry black cats roam around. Hustlers and teenagers stoned on the pale narcotic brew toss them their scraps of shawarma. The precious stones burn crimson and blue in the eyes of Pallas Athena.

JANJA AND THE VULTURE

In a desolate city in the tundra, a capital of bygone days, the buildings of its university still stood. This campus in the city center was falling to ruin: its dull yellow and dreary red stones, the ancient colonnade . . . In spring, frail, tubercular flowers bloomed between stone slabs. Students still showed up sometimes, but there were no entry exams and no sessions, just a few slightly strung-out young men and women gathered in crumbling auditoriums, shivering in the cold, and some professors who looked more like ghosts, sketching on the chalkboards or intoning, in voices hoarse from ceaseless use, something dry and ancient they called knowledge. And those who loved knowledge didn't really understand anything about it, but they loved this dryness and antiquity, like an old book with disintegrating pages from which a little pressed lilac flower suddenly flutters, picked on some unknown day by some unknown hand.

Janja did not come to the university often, but she was respected there, because she *knew*. Her eyes were deep and empty. She would begin speaking quietly, looking beyond the professors and the students and the crumbling auditorium wall—looking beyond the tundra and the sea—and the hearts of those who loved knowledge beat a little faster as they listened to her, though they couldn't understand a word she said. No one knew what Janja was talking about: was she a mathematician, a geometer, a philosopher, a historian? Every manner of thing was mentioned in her talks: numbers and figures, the deeds of the ancients, the wisdom of distant lands.

There was only one thing everybody knew: Janja was fading before their eyes. She was a winter child, and snow seemed to lie along her shining black hair; when summer came, she would melt away. There was no chance that Janja would survive the summer. Her only income came from giving blood, and people don't get healthier that way.

While other students sold drugs or engaged in sex work, Janja gave blood. In the mornings before classes, she went to the disgusting, run-down polyclinic. There she gave blood, and in return received food and money. But her blood was getting worse and worse; from red it had turned to pale pink, and then nearly translucent, and the bones in Janja's body grew so sharp that in several places they began to stick out through her skin. Her left cheekbone protruded, then her collarbone, and then the clinic stopped accepting Janja's blood. They started spitting at her when she showed up there, started beating her with whatever objects were at hand, like a mangy cat, and Janja stopped going. Janja, beautiful winter child! Nothing could save her. But it wasn't Janja who was to be pitied as much as the strange, otherworldly knowledge that lived within her, and through the medium of her wan, monotonous voice brought together in one beautiful, boundless world numbers and figures, humanity's thoughts and deeds, the stones, the grasses, and the stars.

Then summer came, and as she was dying, frail Janja suddenly fell in love. Her beloved was a vulture that had somehow found its way to the tundra and circled above Janja day and night, waiting for her to collapse so it could begin its mourning meal. Maybe it had come from those distant lands that Janja could see with her gaze that penetrated all being. Or maybe she had conjured it from nothing with a look, or disgorged it from within herself, like the hidden death and love that had been growing inside her, and, having finally matured, took on a vulture's form.

The vulture would fly closer and closer, and Janja would weep over it. The vulture also *knew*, just like she did. Their eyes would meet, and the bird's secret wisdom passed into Janja, and Janja wept more and more bitterly. On the day when the frozen sun of the tundra shone a little hotter than usual, and summer warmed the top layer of the earth, Janja undressed and fell into the flowers. The black vulture flew down to Janja and began pecking at her, tenderly and lovingly. Janja trembled and died, giving her body to the bird, and the vulture pecked at her with greater and greater frenzy, at all the wounds of her body, her flesh, her delicate skin. Her knowledge must have passed to the vulture. And then the bird flew far away, to guard this bloody gold.

HUNDREDTH ANNIVERSARY

Two ancient, feeble oldsters are celebrating their wedding anniversary—a hundred years together. The table has been laid in a marshy meadow. Small birds hop along the tablecloth, pecking at crumbs, and there are no guests. In the distance loom the hazy, cloudlike outlines of mountain peaks. The old couple sit at the head of the table and drowse with their eyes open. Their teary, faded eyes see nothing, and only their gnarled, knotted fingers twitch occasionally, resting on the tabletop.

In all their years together they had no children, grandchildren, or great-grandchildren, and their friends have long since died. Now they sit as though carved in stone, and the wind ruffles their white hair. The old woman wears a faded calico dress and a string of beads around her neck; the old man wears a tie and a suit jacket darned at the elbows. We cannot say whether or not they loved each other over the course of their hundred-year union. Perhaps they despised each other. Perhaps now, sitting side by side, they're thinking about how they were always strangers to one another, and remain strangers still. Perhaps the hour of their hundredth anniversary is the hour of their endless loneliness, their lives given to one another in vain. For a hundred years they looked into each other's eyes, until they went blind.

The old woman's lips are pressed into a scornful grimace. The old man sometimes purses his lips and smacks them, like an infant nursing at his mother's breast. A marsh sandpiper whistles sharply, but the couple don't even flinch—they're not only long blind, but have also gone deaf, listening to one another over the course of a hundred years.

And so they sit, with hearts full of love or hate—or, most likely, they're simply exhausted, empty, having long forgotten everything that once made up their lives. A hundred years ago they sat at the head of a table just like this one, and the seats around that table were full, and there was laughter and dancing. But what if they sat then just as they sit now? Frozen, empty eyes staring ahead—as though a century ago, on their wedding day, they were enchanted by trolls. What if they've sat like this for a hundred years without moving, and everyone who knew them died, and nothing remains where their house and their village once stood? And even if they had lived, and moved about, and spoken to one other and to other people, if they worked, ate, slept—wasn't that century a single instant, a fantasy, a dream?

Now they sit here deaf, blind, petrified. Gray geese honk and waddle in the meadow. The gray-brown clouds of the mountains mass in the distance, gold glimmers in the sky, and distant thunder rolls—the trolls are gathering for the celebration.

PET CEMETERY

Two girls—one in a summer dress, the other in shorts and a T-shirt—are biking past a burning lake of oil. The girl in the shorts has an Orlyonok-brand bike, the other one rides a Salute. The bikes' frames are rusty, the brakes barely work, the pedals spin out. The handlebars of the Salute occasionally revolve backwards, and then the girl in the dress has to stop, hold the front tire with her legs, and spin the handlebars back around. The bare legs of the girl in shorts are covered in scratches and black marks from the bike chain. Riding over scorched earth, they suddenly freeze: far off but visible, coming from the direction of the burning lake and running like mad, there's a frightened, solitary deer.

"Shh," one girl says to the other, putting a finger to her lips. Then they ride on. The soil beneath their wheels bears the permanent-seeming impress of some continuous-track vehicle.

"Turn left," says the girl in the dress. "There it is."

Before them is a low hill covered in sun-bleached deer moss, with a little wooden door leading inside. There's a lock on the door—gnomes live here. Next to the hill is a concrete circle in the earth, with a hole at its center. It's an old well, but there's no water left. The girls leave their bikes by the hill and walk on.

A wooden post has been hammered into the earth, and a sign hangs from the post: Pet Cemetery. A grave outlined in bricks, little stones tossed in, a black marble sign proclaiming: Dina the Dog. A bouquet of blackened artificial flowers, a picture of a guinea pig: Djorik. The black dog Salmochka, her grave surrounded by a fence. The gravestone says, "Why did you leave us? We grieve and remember you." Siberian cat Ferik looks out from a photograph, squinting wisely. There were once many flowers here; now only stone slabs remain, and fences and faded photographs. The girl in the dress wipes away a tear. The girl in shorts says, "I just don't understand it."

THE ICON PAINTER AND THE DOG-HEADED MAN

Icon painter Alypius, long-haired and bearded, with a gaze that is not of this world, stands shooting geese, knee-deep in bobtails at the edge of the lake. All around there's only sedge and cotton grass. Tearing through the dwarf birches, he drags the goose he has shot toward his hut. It's a fat, meaty bird, five kilos at least. Alypius is pleased. His ancestors came here to get away from the Antichrist, but they all died out a long time ago, Alypius is the only one left. Once upon a time, one of the strange, alien folks who used to live in these parts came to him and stayed: a dog-headed man. A hulk with the head of a dog. Alypius paints Saint Christopher in his likeness—doggy profile, ochre halo, warrior breastplate, pitch-black background. Alypius depicts him with his spear and shield, holding a sprig of creeping Arctic willow.

The dog-headed man sits by their hut smoking a pipe.

"Get a goose?" he asks.

"Got one," says Alypius, drops the goose, sits beside him. The pipe smoke keeps away some of the mosquitoes and other little bugs. Slowly, hazily, they look out at the field of dwarf birch and moss, at the lake, at the low grasses.

"Saw a grebe on the lake today," says the icon painter. "Such a pretty one—two little horns on its head, crest between them, red eyes."

"I had a dream today that people came here asking to be fed, but then I woke up—and there was no one there."

"Eh, brother, nobody's ever going to come here. No one's come here in my whole life. Since my mother died thirty-some years ago, I haven't seen one other person, except you, dog-head."

"Better they don't come, then. And there probably aren't any people left, anyhow."

"No one's around, that's for sure."

They cook the goose, say a prayer, sit down to supper. Then they go down to sleep for the night on their wooden bedsteads. Before he sleeps, Alypius recites his prayers, while the dog-headed man thinks to himself, "Why does he do that, doesn't he understand that if all the people are gone, God's gone, too? Or is God hanging on just because of Alypius here? Maybe that's how it is," thinks the dog-headed man. It's definitely not because of *him*, he's not really Saint Christopher, after all, the one who carried God on his back. The dog-headed man listens to the many mixed-up fragments of thoughts rippling through his mind and becoming dreams. Here, in the middle of the tundra, he sees a post, and there's a rope tied to the post, and the rope's frayed end trembles in the wind . . .

A little lamp smokes in the corner before an image of Jesus. Alypius sleeps knowing that the icon will keep him safe from the Antichrist and from the wolves. The dog-headed man sleeps, and in his sleep hears Alypius breathing, and knows that even if there is no God, he himself will protect Alypius from the polar darkness, heavy melancholy, and endless loneliness.

DANDELIONS

By the bombed-out missile silos, giant dandelions have grown, tall as a five-year-old child. Out of the boundless grasses their stems rise up, full of bitter milk, nodding and swaying the enormous golden orbs of their sentient heads.

"Why are we so big?" one dandelion asks another.

"Probably because of the radiation," the other tells him.

The sun-bright weave of their buds conceals a sticky dandelion honey, jelly with a bitter tinge, wine. Slowly they transform, changing into a fine flickering web, donning the delicate celestial netting of their seeds. At night, they don't fold up their flowers, don't go to sleep as their brethren used to do, but glow, like huge flowery moons. Gradually, in June, the dandelions lose their minds: all their reason goes into their seeds, but the seeds blow away with the wind, and with each flown silver-white puff, a dandelion loses a part of its soul. Many of them stand there for some time, half-mad, others—still only a quarter crazy, but sooner or later all the seeds have flown and every dandelion loses what's left of its mind and soul. You could say that now it has become a plant. Or that it has acute diminished motivation syndrome. With no expression whatever, their emptied centers gaze into the sky, heads pocked with the little dots to which their seeds had clung so loosely. Yes, they may have lost themselves, but they've succeeded in scattering their souls over the fields and grasses. Dispersed in thousands of puffs, their souls will find themselves new shelter in the soil, their countless children will rise as furious suns, full of honey and wine, and they will inherit the earth.

PALACE OF THE ANGELS

Far away, in the distant mountains, they say there is a palace or castle at the very top of a steep peak—the trees stretch their boughs toward it and the swan-clouds stretch their wings. There's warmth and food there, and hope and happiness; every day, there's a ball for dancing and a hunt on horseback. Angels live there, and they take in anyone who reaches them.

They say there once was a girl who went into the forest in winter, a kingfisher showing her the way. She walked among white, green, violet, and blue trees, and she found apple trees laden with winter apples. Stars dusted with snow fell into the forest, and the girl saw by the light of their glow. These stars could be gathered and eaten, and they tasted sweet, like chilled berry juice. This girl walked all the way to the castle, and now she'll be happy there forever.

There was another young woman, too, who had no hands. Her hands had been chopped off and eaten by cannibals. Once she had a dream about a palace with bright windows and a wonderful garden, where there was a waterfall and a stone grotto. She dreamed of a rider in a crimson cape astride a golden steed, and she dreamed of an emerald bird. She set out, and she saw the birds and the apple tree, and she met one of the angels, who took a liking to her and brought her to the palace. There she sleeps on a downy feather bed that gets fluffed each morning, behind an emerald canopy, and she's grown a new set of hands.

Once, a pair of siblings set out to find the castle. The brother and sister crossed rivers, ate tree bark, and passed the ruins of cities everywhere. Traveling through the tundra, they met a lady—a queen from the Hyperborean branch of the Hapsburgs. Gaunt as hunger itself, she always went about naked, only covering her hair with a long bath towel that hung down her back. She kept a fire going in her stove, which stood in the middle of the tundra, in the spot where her house once was. Now only the stove remained, as well as a large cauldron for making food, two clay pots, a pitcher, and a stool. Near the stove stood two barrels of water. In the earth, there was a cellar where the queen kept her grain and human-meat provisions. She slept on the grass, naked, beneath the scant sun, and her favorite thing to do was watch the clouds as they turned pink. In those moments, it seemed to her that harsh, angry thoughts fled from her mind like eagle owls, hooting and flying into the past.

The brother and sister went on, dreaming of the things they would have.

"I'll have a dog and a cat," said the boy. "And a brand-new bike."

"I'm going to have my own little house," said the girl, "a cozy little house. In winter the roof will be all covered with snow, and the windows will glow with light, and it'll be warm inside and smell like Grandmother's pies."

"I'm going to grow up and meet a beautiful lady," said the boy. "I'll wear a frock coat and she'll wear a silk dress. And we'll walk together in the garden, among tall trees."

"And I'm going to stand by a window," said the girl, "waiting for my beloved. He'll be dressed in gold and ride up on a golden horse. And I'll be the most beautiful girl in the world."

They talked like this for a long time: We're going to drink tea with cinnamon, we're going to eat cheesecake, we're going to go to McDonald's, we'll go to the movies to see *Batman* . . . And they walked and walked and grew so tired that they couldn't walk any longer. They lay down in the snow, and for a long time told each other about the things they would have, until they froze to death.

But on the winter trees around them giant apples grew, and snow-dusted stars tumbled from the sky, riders cavorted on golden horses, and emerald birds soared. The angels found the siblings and brought them to their palace, where they breathed life into them and gave them everything they desired, and more. They gave the children a dog, a cat, a parrot, and a pair of little ponies; they gave them racing bikes and a little winter cabin that smelled like Grandmother's pies, and the most delicious tea and cheesecake, and McDonald's meals, and a *Batman* film; they promised them beautiful beloveds when they grew up. And the angels gave them an iPad, an iPod, and an iPhone.

DAEDALLA

There once was a wooden doll who lived in the tundra city of Knossos. No one else lived there, only venomous centipedes, because the city's old tsar had been wont to ejaculate centipedes when he lay with women. The tsar was dead, the women were dead too, but the centipedes remained. The tsar had been in Hell for quite some time, now in the form of a demon with a serpent's tail, which he wound around newly arriving souls, but a single wooden doll—she had been his doll—continued wandering alone through the remains of his palace.

Not just his, but all the palaces of the tundra had burned: the palaces of Knossos, and Phaistos, and Zakros. Fires scorched the palaces and the deer moss around them, the poppies and buttercups, the rockfoil and lousewort. Then ash and goose-down floated down from the skies and blanketed everything. The wooden doll had burned too, but she had been made by a great craftsman, so she survived the flames, though she grew dark as coal. Now the doll wandered the palace halls, and it seemed to her that the ruins of the palace were her own mind, hollowed out by the elements.

In the old days, the doll had sung and composed poems, but she couldn't do that any longer; the fires had burned all of that to ashes. The doll entered storage rooms for grain and wine, but the vessels there were empty. She wandered the megaron, where figure-eight shields were painted on the walls. She ascended via a narrow corridor from the columned hall to the central courtyard; she passed through open spaces and darkened rooms, went down halls and staircases, past courtyards and colonnades. In some places, fragments of frescoes remained, depicting processions and deer hunts, berry-gathering, snow sheep and wolves, lemmings and polar owls, the tundra's spring efflorescence, through which strolled ladies with wasp-thin waists, in lightblue and pomegranate-red dresses with magnificent hoop skirts. Gryphons were carved on both sides of the throne in the throne room, and around them were polar forget-me-nots against a red background. All the columns in the palace narrowed toward their base.

The doll was searching for someone concealed at the center of this labyrinth, someone who was the secret she kept in her own heart. But all the rooms stood empty, and the center was empty too, and the doll understood that there was no longer any secret in her heart. The doll stood at the center of palace, looking around wildly.

Once upon a time, a great craftsman had made her for the tsar who ejaculated centipedes in the act of love, so that he could lie with the doll instead of harming living women. Like a woman, she had an opening between her legs. The doll's mind and heart were empty now, they'd been burned to ashes, and this emptiness inside tormented her. She picked up the centipedes crawling around and thrust them between her legs. She thrust and thrust until she was completely filled with centipedes.

The doll had once been called Daedalus after the great craftsman who made her, but, because she was a female doll, she called herself Daedalla.

GHOST TRAIN

Along the sun-scorched earth of the tundra, past the crude oil pipeline, runs a set of trolley tracks, and down the tracks rolls a trolley of many cars, a hundred cars all linked together, the train stretches to the horizon and there is no end to it. All of the cars are empty except one, but electric lights blaze in all of them. The train runs past puddles of muddy water that aren't quite lakes, past shriveled shrubs, past heaps of garbage. From time to time there are dead deer on the tracks, and then the train comes to a stop, and the driver, cursing, gets out and drags them to the side. Electric streetlamps line the tracks, and the season's first snowflakes twirl in their light, even though it's the middle of July. In the gloom of the cloudy white night, the shadows of the odd fox or hare flicker in places where the lamplight doesn't reach.

The train is driven by a driver in a tunic and cap. His face is simple and sly, there's a web of wrinkles beneath his squinting eyes, he's got protruding ears and a weedy little orange beard. He was born an orphan and became a Red driver, and now he drives the trolley train and thinks, gazing ahead into the unknown, "Oh tundra, tundra, you enchanted realm, Great October brought you a new destiny. You submitted to the Soviet man. We'll mine for ore here, and for oil and gas, we'll build power plants, processing centers, chemical and metallurgical factories, cities and towns."

Only one car of the hundred is full: inside it ride the conductor, the tsar, and the tsaritsa. The tsaritsa sits by the window, the tsar next to her.

"Look, it's starting to snow," the tsar says. "Like we're coming home from the theater in Petersburg, and snow is falling in the light of the lamps."

The conductor sits and watches them without blinking. She's an old lady, long braid down her back. Her eyes are leucoma-white and the wrinkles on her forehead make her look a touch astonished. She's dressed in a black dress with a brooch. Her name's Dearie-Death-Aglaia-Filippovna.

They pass a lake of burning oil. The tsaritsa gasps and nudges the tsar: What a travesty.

"It's like that everywhere now," says Dearie-Death-Aglaia-Filippovna. "The deer are dying, all the deer are dying nowadays, and where are your tickets?" The tsar and tsaritsa show her their contactless smartcards.

"Shall we have a nip of vodka?" asks Dearie-Death-Aglaia-Filippovna. The tsar and tsaritsa agree. They have a drink, they have another drink, the tsar looks through the window, and he thinks: "Oh tundra, tundra, you enchanted realm . . ." There's a heavy, painful-sorrowful feeling in his heart.

The train stops at the top of an embankment, the doors open, Dearie-Death-Aglaia-Filippovna makes the sign of the cross over the tsar and the tsaritsa in farewell. The Chekist secret police meet the tsar and the tsaritsa and take them down to the foot of the embankment, shoot them, and bury them there. The train moves on without any passengers. The driver rolls himself a cigarette. Dearie-Death-Aglaia-Filippovna pours herself another shot. The Chekists by the embankment watch the cars of the trolley train passing. The cars are brightly lit by the electric lights, they're all empty, and they roll on for a long, long time, alike as twins, passing over the cold, perishing alien soil of the tundra. The first snow falls on the Chekists' uniforms, bringing with it a sense of aching, lingering solitude. Suddenly, from the shifting tundra shadows, a deer emerges, with a spot on its forehead a bit like a five-pointed star. Coming up behind the Chekist who oversaw the execution, it rests its head on his shoulder.

THE SKEPTICAL CAT

A Dark Fairy Tale About the Destruction of Paradise

Orphaned children and mechanical dolls walked through the tundra, and a stuffed cat named Barsik led them. They were on their way to build a city where humans, machines, plants, and animals could dwell together in peace. They were dressed in rags and struggled to make their way through the cold, until, finally, they reached the shore of a great sea and founded their city. They called the city New London.

The little vagrants and intelligent machines divided the city's jobs between them: some became mechanical engineers, others heating engineers, others hydraulic engineers. Some became mad scientists and others became madmen; some went to work as detectives and others as spies; still others decided to be revolutionaries. The population split up into capitalists and the proletariat. The girls formed two factions: prostitutes and feminists. They laid out cobblestone streets, put up gas lamps, opened shops. They built steam-powered dreadnaughts and piloted dirigibles. Barsik, the stuffed cat, moved into a palace in the center of the city and had dominion over all. Deer, wolves, and snow sheep also came to the city to live alongside the humans and the machines, as did various plants: creeping Arctic willow, dwarf birches, shrubs of different kinds. And all dwelled there in peace and harmony: *no shit happened.*

The problems, when they began, came from all sides. The machines rose up against the humans and used steam-powered tanks to occupy the city's central square. Then the animals rose up against the humans too, and started eating them, and the plants rose up against the humans and starting pricking and scratching them. The animals also began eating each other—the wolves attacked the deer, the foxes attacked the rabbits, and the plants fought amongst themselves using their roots. The mad scientists invented the atomic bomb and started threatening everyone with it; the madmen resolved to murder the entire populace; the spies kept foreign powers appraised of these events and the foreign powers sent in their agents. The capitalists began to brutally oppress the proletariat, at which point the revolutionaries revolted. The prostitutes gave everyone HIV, and the feminists came out against the men. The city was shelled from the dirigibles and the dreadnoughts, and no one could step foot outside without a revolver, rifle, or Gatling gun. The orphan children had long since grown up, and many had had children of their own, so an orphanage was built for their kids, since the mothers were either militant feminists or prostitutes and both groups were too busy to bring up children. It was the war of all against all. And then in secret, with a bindle over his shoulder, Barsik the cat quit the city.

He walked alone through the tundra as spring arrived, and buttercups, rockfoil, and milkvetch began to bloom. There was a bow on his chest, little markings on his plush coat. His blue gimlet eyes gazed into the distance that spread out before him. He no longer had any faith in people, machines, plants, or animals. Far off behind him, a large mushroom cloud was rising into the sky. And that is how Barsik the stuffed cat became a skeptic.

BASTINDA'S WRITING GROUP

Hope

In a capital of bygone days, a tundra city forsaken by gods and men, built on barren earth sown with bitter memories, there was an orphanage. It was an ordinary, simple brick building surrounded by a garden with a swing set. In the garden grew moss and nothing else. The children at the orphanage weren't abused—they were just left to their own devices, fed watery soup. During the darker seasons the children rarely went outside, but it was also cold indoors, so they burned the furniture to keep warm. The city had a ramshackle porn studio, and occasionally people came to the orphanage to make their movies, and the kids got sticky candies for doing it. There was also a writing group at the orphanage, run by a mad poetess named Bastinda.

Nobody knew exactly how Bastinda taught the young orphans the art of poetry, but by the age of fifteen all the children at the orphanage had matured into genius poets. They knew *The Iliad* and *The Odyssey* by heart; they could read and translate Virgil, Ovid, and Catullus; they wrote poems using complex classical meters and invented new ones, and every child produced poetry that was a world unto itself, each unlike any of the others. The orphans didn't know or care to know much about life outside the orphanage; their poems were pure knowledge independent of experience. They demanded only one thing of their verse—that it soar—and they had mastered this art to perfection. Just as blind nightingales sing more sweetly than sighted ones, the children wrote their poems ignorant of everything that existed, not knowing love or childhood, strangers to the barren earth and the bitterness of life. But even that impoverished earth could bring forth sacred dreams. The children took on pseudonyms based on the names of birds: Longspur Laplandsky, Pacifica Plover, Red Pipit.

The year when they were released "into adult life" from the orphanage, Bastinda died, and the writing group disbanded. Beyond the walls of the orphanage, in the ruined city, the children had nowhere to go. Nobody had any use for these young men and women with their dispassionate gazes, or for their poetry. Some of them died, because life offered them nothing, and rather threatened to take away the little they had. Longspur learned to cook up a pale narcotic brew and sold it in a tent at the market on the shore of the icy sea. Pacifica and Red went to work at the porn studio.

Many of the young orphans stopped writing poetry, but Longspur, Pacifica, and Red kept going, and sometimes their poems appeared in the city's only literary magazine, put out by an old eccentric who considered this his life's work. The magazine was published once every seven years on clumsily pasted-together sheets of fragile, yellowing paper, in a run of seven issues, which were all ritually torn apart and scattered over the sea unread, and it was called *Hope*.

TRANSLATOR'S ACKNOWLEDGMENTS

I'm grateful to Daniel Kipnis, Daniel Lefferts, and Jessi Jezewska Stevens for their thoughts on these translations; to Will Evans, Sarah McEachern, Linda Stack-Nelson, and everyone else at Deep Vellum; to the Banke, Goumen & Smirnova Literary Agency; to Irina Gachechiladze. Enormous thanks to Alla Gorbunova, for entrusting me with her work.

Earlier versions of "Biomass," "The Life of Shagdarov," and "In the Sight of Athena" appeared in the *New England Review*. Versions of "Act of Nature," "Oy Oy Oy," and "ἐκπύρωσις" appeared in *Words Without Borders*. A version of "Dandelions" appeared in the *Nashville Review*. I'm grateful to the editors of these publications, and to the Lighthouse Works Residency and the Hawthornden Foundation for their support.

The translation of *Things and Thoughts* is made possible in part by the New York State Council on the Arts with the support of the Office of the Governor and the New York State Legislature.

Alla Gorbunova has published seven books of poetry and six books of prose. Her novel *It's the End of the World, My Love*, was awarded the NOS Prize, and the poetry collection *Inside Starfall* received the Andrey Bely Prize. Her work has been translated into over a dozen languages.

Elina Alter is a writer and the translator of Alla Gorbunova's *It's the End of the World, My Love*. Her other translations include Oksana Vasyakina's *Wound* and *Steppe*.